THE VIKING SHE LOVES TO HATE

Lucy Morris

MILLS & BOON

First published in Great Britain 2023
by Mills & Boon, an imprint of HarperCollins*Publishers* Ltd,
1 London Bridge Street, London, SE1 9GF

www.harpercollins.co.uk

HarperCollins*Publishers*, Macken House, 39/40 Mayor Street Upper,
Dublin 1, D01 C9W8, Ireland

The Viking She Loves to Hate © 2023 Lucy Morris

ISBN: 978-0-263-30529-6

07/23

MIX
Paper | Supporting responsible forestry
FSC
www.fsc.org
FSC™ C007454

This book is produced from independently certified FSC™ paper to ensure responsible forest management.
For more information visit: www.harpercollins.co.uk/green.

Printed and Bound in the UK using 100% Renewable Electricity at CPI Group (UK) Ltd, Croydon, CR0 4YY

Also by Lucy Morris

The Viking Chief's Marriage Alliance
A Nun for the Viking Warrior

Shieldmaiden Sisters miniseries

The Viking She Would Have Married
Tempted by Her Outcast Viking
Beguiling Her Enemy Warrior

Discover more at millsandboon.co.uk.

Lucy Morris lives in Essex, UK, with her husband, two young children and two cats. She has a massively sweet tooth and loves gin, bubbly and Irn-Bru. She's a member of the UK Romantic Novelists' Association, and was delighted when Mills & Boon accepted her manuscript after she'd submitted her story to the Warriors Wanted! blitz for Viking, Medieval and Highlander romances. Writing for Mills & Boon Historical is a dream come true for her, and she hopes you enjoy her books!

For the boy I could never hate, my son Rory.

Chapter One

Northern Fjords, AD 830

It was *too* perfect, and that worried Ulrik more than any storm or battle ever could. Good fortune had never been a close companion of his, and he wondered why the gods would favour him now.

'Welcome to my kingdom!' said King Viggo as he slapped him heartily on the back with an affable smile. 'I hope you and your daughter will be happy here.'

'Thank you, my lord. I am sure we will,' Ulrik replied with a respectful bow, but Viggo was already jumping down from the longship and onto the settlement's jetty before the words had even left his mouth.

The King must have seen over fifty winters, but he had the strength and vitality of a much younger man. Time had been kind to the King, but wasn't that always the way of things? Viggo still had a strong body and a laugh that boomed like thunder. The only physical difference was that Viggo's red hair and beard were now streaked with veins of white and gold, but otherwise he was as wild and as boisterous as he had been when they had first met during the western raids.

Who would have thought that Ulrik would ever meet him again, or be offered a position as the King's master boat-builder? Despite the long journey, Ulrik was still numb from the shock of it.

Frida gave him a bright smile, and he squeezed his daughter's hand as he helped her off the boat. No matter his own misgivings, he did not want her to worry. This was her dream, and he would not fail her a second time.

'It is beautiful!' gasped Frida as she stared wide-eyed at the spectacular fjord surrounding them. The ocean water gleamed an emerald-green in its centre, then bled out to a dusky blue along the coastline. The settlement was grand, with many colourful houses and workshops.

Lush forests covered the mountain ranges surrounding them, their rocky peaks topped with frost. They encircled the flat farmlands of the settlement and harbour as if they were a mother's arms protecting them from the elements. Not that the weather was harsh—the spring sunshine bathed the land in a golden light, pushing winter firmly into the shadows of memory.

The King looked as if he were about to leave without saying anything more. So Ulrik limped after him, trying his best to ignore the increasingly sharp, stabbing pain that raced down his thigh. The voyage had meant he'd been unable to stretch it properly, and now he would suffer for it. 'King Viggo, is that my workshop further down the beach—shall I row our things there?'

'Call me Viggo!' laughed the King, brushing away the formality as if it were a troublesome fly. 'All my trusted men do. You will be staying in the hall tonight. Until I can sort out your lodgings.' Frowning, Viggo glanced at the old fishing boat still tied to his ship. Ulrik had insisted on bringing it with them. It was filled with his tools and covered in a waxed canvas. 'You can collect that later. When your position here is confirmed.'

Unease squirmed in Ulrik's belly reminding him that nothing was ever guaranteed in this world. 'I thought you said you needed a new master boatbuilder?' If that was not the case, he was very glad to still have his fishing boat. An ocean voyage would be impossible, but he could at least use it to travel back down the coast to Aalborg...not that there was anything for them there. They had given it all up to travel here.

When would he ever learn?

He should not take such risks, especially when it came to Frida's future. But Viggo had seemed so genuine with his offer of a new life. Grateful even... It seemed strange that he would now be so uncertain.

'I will...soon enough,' Viggo replied lightly, although worryingly he didn't meet Ulrik's eyes. 'Now, I must go and greet my wife, before she poisons my mead for keeping her waiting.'

Viggo strode away, greeted by the welcoming cheers of his people. That at least boded well. Viggo was not a tyrant, but was he a liar?

Rubbing his bad leg, Ulrik tried to recall the warrior he had known all those years ago. Mischievous, determined, and ruthless were the words that came to mind. Not necessarily bad traits in a man, and surely he would keep his word?

One day I will repay you.

Ulrik had saved Viggo's life once, and had been badly wounded in the process, an injury that still plagued him daily.

It spoke well for the King that he remembered it. Viggo had not forgotten his promise despite the many years that had passed since. In fact, he had seemed genuinely delighted to meet him again. Especially when he had learned Ulrik was a boat-builder with ambitions to run his own shipyard one day. Immediately Viggo had offered him a master's position in his homeland. It was an opportunity someone like Ulrik could not refuse.

Why, then, had Viggo been so vague?

Did he really need a boat-builder? His current ship was exceptionally well-crafted. Ulrik had seen that for himself when he had repaired its minor damages caused by a storm. The craftsman who had originally designed and built it was equal in skill to Ulrik—so why would Viggo need another?

Now that he was here, Ulrik could see the large shipyard and workshops further down the shingle beach that must belong to the current builder. It did not look abandoned or closed—in fact, smoke streamed from one chimney and he could see several figures moving around the shipyard at work. There were large timber hoists and pulleys, as well as scaffolding frames that although currently empty did not look old or in disrepair.

'Father?' Frida whispered quietly, drawing his attention back to her.

Her hair had unravelled from her braid a little, the dark strands dancing around her face in the breeze, and she brushed at them absently with her free hand.

The other clutched her meagre sack of possessions, her small knuckles white against the brown cloth.

He prayed to all the gods that he had not taken her from Aalborg foolishly. Their previous home hadn't been as beautiful or as prosperous as this, but it had paid a regular income, even if it hadn't been earned as the master builder.

No, he could not fail in this endeavour and this opportunity had come at the best of times. Frida would be a grown woman in only a few short years, the softness of her childhood fading as her beauty sharpened.

Recently, she had started to remind him of Sigrid, the similarity of their expressions so painfully close that sometimes it hurt to look at her. Thankfully that was where the resemblance to her mother ended. Her colouring was like his, hair as dark as wet earth and blue eyes the same colour as the deep water of this fjord.

Frida would need a dowry eventually. One good enough to entice a strong and worthy husband for her. Someone who could finally give her the life she deserved. He would never earn enough in Aalborg... he barely earned enough to feed them through the winter as it was.

He gently took the sack from her, and picked up his own from the jetty floor where he had left it. 'Come,

let us go to the hall. I am sure we will find a place
for our things soon.'

Her gaze shifted towards the distant shipyard, and
then returned to his with a weak smile. Frida was
quick-witted, she would realise the same thing he had,
and he could tell it made her nervous.

Who could fault her for it?

Her life had been filled with uncertainty, and he
was the one to blame for it. He only hoped he had not
made a terrible mistake in coming here.

Perhaps the current boat-builder was leaving soon,
or had fallen out of favour with the King? Whatever
Viggo's reasons for replacing them, Ulrik did not care.
He only hoped that he and Frida would remain.

Cheers rang out across the hall as Astrid's father
made yet another toast. The answering shouts of
agreement from his people shook the dust from the
rafters. The feast was at its peak, with drunken men
already swaying in their seats, as more platters of
food and ale were brought out by her mother's thralls.

Astrid stood in the shadows, and allowed herself a
moment to enjoy the sight before the night was spoiled
by her presence.

Her father went trading often, and was gone for
many months at a time. But when he was home it
felt as if life were bursting with colour and noise,

after months of gloom. There were luxurious gifts handed out, and so much feasting that people forgot what day it was.

Astrid missed him when he was gone, or at least she had used to. Missed his laugh, and the way he seemed unable to speak in any tone lower than a shout, especially when he was deep in his cups like now. As a child she had loved his feasts, watching from beneath tables. Whittling toys from scraps of wood, and secretly tying the men's leg wraps together, so that when they stumbled and fell it would make her father laugh even louder. But that was when she was younger, before she became a woman. Then her tricks became unseemly, and her carvings were looked at with resentment and irritation.

She had lost her father's favour by merely remaining the same. Now when he returned she felt as if she was fighting an endless war. Except for in these golden moments before he noticed her, and she could reminisce about the old days.

Soon he would wrestle with his men, or start singing in that rich and throaty voice of his, spilling ale on the rushes as he wove between the tables.

Her father was a King well-loved by his people. She was sure her brother, when he eventually came to power, would be similar in nature. They took after each other so thoroughly, even down to the fiery colour of their hair. All Viggo's children had red hair except Astrid, whose dark hair only carried a few strands of flame.

However, unlike their older sisters, Astrid and her brother shared Viggo's rebellious and adventurous nature...although Viggo only travelled with his son, something Astrid had envied until she had found her own happiness in her carpentry.

Her mother, Inga, sat beside the King, her back stiff and straight, her smooth blonde hair woven in an intricate style that showed off her slender neck and the gold that adorned it. She always seemed so awkward with him, especially in the first few days of his return. But then, her father was absent so often that it must feel to her mother as if a cuckoo had settled in her nest.

Viggo began to recount a tale from his recent travels, his commanding voice filling the room, and silencing the chatter.

'We fought the serpents of the sea. My strong boy and I...' Viggo grinned, nodding towards Astrid's brother, who rolled his eyes good-naturedly. He was as tall as their father and just as broad. As the only son, he also carried Viggo's name and was known by everyone as 'Viggo the Younger'. Except by Astrid and their father, who called him 'Boy', although in recent years Viggo had added 'Strong', so as not to shame him. Astrid refused to do the same purely out of sisterly spite...

'But they were too fierce and threatened to snap our keel in two.'

Astrid shifted away from the pillar she had been leaning against. Her pride and interest had been caught on her father's hook, drawing her out of the shadows and into the light. She had not noticed any serious damage to her father's ship when she had passed it earlier. But maybe she should check it over in the morning, as she did not want her father to have any excuse to question her skill as the master boat-builder.

Viggo gestured to the man sitting at a bench in front of the King's table. 'We made safe harbour at Aalborg, where I was reunited with an old friend.'

The man had dark brown hair, tied back with intricate braids that seemed to be the only attempt this man had taken in caring for his appearance. Astrid noticed a young girl of about thirteen or fourteen winters beside him who had similarly styled hair. Had she braided it? Was he a brother or father perhaps?

Astrid could not be certain of his age, because he had a thick beard that covered most of his face. She would guess he was not that old, however, as there wasn't a single strand of white in his dark hair, and he was powerfully built. Over wide, muscular shoulders he wore a threadbare tunic that should have been turned into cleaning rags months ago. He wore no cloak or brooch adornment, but held his head high as he looked towards the King.

Poor but strong.

Why would her father favour such a warrior?

Her silent question was immediately answered, as her father said, 'Ulrik is a master boat-builder who repaired my ship so well that *Dragon's Breath* is now even swifter than she was before.'

A replacement!

It made sense, and yet, as always, it still hurt. Hot anger and jealousy struck down her spine, causing her to step out into the middle of the room. Now she knew the real reason why her father had brought this man here. She had refused to marry anyone, and now her father would take away her livelihood. Without it, she would be left with nothing, and her father knew that. But rather than take it away himself, he had brought a usurper here instead, to swallow her dreams whole, and call it an act of friendship.

She would never allow it!

'Impossible!' she snapped. 'How could he make it better, with only simple repairs? She was perfectly sound before leaving here, and has returned with only a few new planks and nails…hardly the work of a master!'

The man's eyes shifted slowly to hers, and she was paralysed for a moment by their vivid colour. So startling in his otherwise unassuming face...and cold, absent of all emotion. She wondered how this soulless wretch had managed to worm his way into her father's heart.

'It can't,' Ulrik replied, his voice so deep it rattled her bones. 'It can only support what was already there.'

It took her a long moment to realise he was agreeing with her.

What sort of game was he trying to play?

Unless he feared her status as a princess... But he didn't look afraid. He looked strong, and powerful, confident in every word he uttered, and for some reason it made her stomach flip in a disturbing way.

How dare he glare at her with such bitter resentment?

She was the wounded party here, not him. She had worked hard for many years to learn the skills needed to be a master boat-builder. Viggo had been so impressed by the first ship she'd built that he had named it *Dragon's Breath*, and called it his greatest treasure.

Her father gave a casual shrug, even as he avoided her condemning eyes. 'Well, it certainly felt a swifter journey on the return. Smoother too, as if our prow were cutting the waves like a hot knife through butter. I was very impressed. Now, Astrid, my darling girl, I would like you to meet the man responsible— Ulrik Leifsson…he is a—'

'I heard,' she snapped, interrupting her father with a brittle glare. 'Why would you invite a boat-builder here? Especially when you already *have* one?' Astrid strode forward towards the King's table, people moving out of her way, sensing the Princess's displeasure.

Deliberately she ignored the piercing eyes of the strange man as she passed him, and made her way to her father. She kissed Viggo's cheek stiffly in welcome, before taking her seat.

Viggo seemed content to ignore her question, and instead frowned at her manly attire. 'I thought I said to dress appropriately in the hall.'

Her mother leaned elegantly forward in her seat. 'She usually does. However, I am sure Astrid was so pleased by your safe return that she forgot to change.'

'Yes, Father. Whenever I eat here, I always wear my gowns,' Astrid said, failing to mention that she rarely ate in the hall, as she preferred to eat and drink on the beach with her friends most nights. The only rule her mother insisted on was for her to join her for dagmal each morning.

She gave her mother a grateful smile. Inga had always been a surprising champion of her unfeminine behaviour, keeping the worst of it from her father's eyes and ears.

However, Viggo did not fail to see the weighted look pass between mother and daughter, and he sipped from his horn of ale with a sour expression. When next he spoke, his voice was unusually lowered, his words meant for their ears only. 'Astrid, you will never get a husband if you keep dressing and behaving like a man.'

'What a pity,' Astrid replied cheerfully as she heaped her platter with bread, pickles and roasted meats.

'Both of your sisters are married, and have been content for some time now,' Viggo grumbled, and Astrid knew immediately where this miserable conversation was headed. 'Surely you do not wish to spend your life alone?'

No, but I would rather that than a single day of your marriage, thought Astrid, although she dared not say it.

Their constant bickering was a lesson she had taken to heart.

'She is our youngest daughter—let her enjoy her freedom for a little longer.' Inga smiled indulgently, delicately placing a spoonful of braised apple and cabbage on Astrid's platter, her favourite side-dish. 'There is plenty of time to find the perfect match for her.'

'She has seen over five and twenty winters, Inga! She needs to marry, and soon. Even as my daughter it will be a struggle to find a man willing to take on such an old bride.'

'Old!' Inga's eyes turned to ice. 'If my daughter is old, then what am I?'

'A beloved wife and mother.' Viggo glared at her. 'And do not turn this into an argument as you usually do.'

'Why should I marry?' interrupted Astrid. 'You have two daughters who have made good alliances for you already, as well as an heir to your throne.'

'You need to start a family of your own. For too long you have run around, idly doing whatever you please! You need protection and a purpose in life.'

'I have both! I am your master boat-builder and I am under your protection.'

'I am sure we could find you a husband that allowed you to continue your carving… That is what you truly enjoy is it not, being an artisan?'

Astrid scowled. 'I enjoy both aspects.'

Years ago she had argued that boat-building was an artisan's craft when her father had objected to her learning it from their aging boat-builder. Now he was using that argument against her. Her father wasn't just a king because he was well-loved, there was intelligence and ruthlessness behind those cheerful smiles.

'Well, my good friend Ulrik is here now, and I owe him a great debt.'

Astrid frowned. 'A debt?'

Duty *and* friendship would be used against her!

'He saved my life once many years ago, took an axe in the thigh meant for me. It is fortunate we meet again after all these years. I can finally repay him.'

'And so you now give a stranger *my position!*' Her voice rose with indignation. 'How do you even know if he can build a ship? He only repaired the one that *I* made!'

'I can build you a ship, faster than any other,' came the booming voice of Ulrik. She had not realised he had been following their conversation from afar. The hall quietened and she cursed the man for interfering in what was obviously a family matter.

'See!' Viggo cheered, and raised his horn to toast Ulrik. 'And that is what I truly need. A fast ship, with plenty of cargo room. As beautiful as your carvings are—'

'My ships are both beautiful and functional!' Astrid shouted in outrage, although she felt like that little girl caught causing mischief beneath the tables.

Inga nodded, placing a calming hand on her arm. 'Viggo, you said yourself that *Dragon's Breath* is your pride and joy. You even said to bury you in it when your time came.'

'It is a beauty,' Viggo conceded, 'but perhaps Ulrik could build me something better in the future?'

'In the future? Your time in this world might be shorter than you think, *my love,'* hissed Inga under her breath.

Viggo gave a gruff snort of amusement and then spoke loudly for all to hear. 'Perhaps a competition, then? To see who can build the best ship.'

Astrid felt dread pool in her stomach. Surely her father wasn't going to do this? But it appeared he was, because Ulrik sat up taller in his seat and called out, 'I will take part in any *fair* contest of skill.'

The way that he had said the word *fair* irritated her. It implied that he thought there might be some impartiality on her father's part. It would have made Astrid howl with laughter if she hadn't been so furious.

'You think my father an unfair judge?' she asked in disbelief.

Her father judging the contest would be more of a hindrance than a help to her. Viggo seemed determined to ruin her life. But then again...

Maybe she could use Ulrik's fears to aid her own cause?

As long as her father was not the judge, there was still a chance...

'I know well what a man would do for his daughter,' replied Ulrik coldly, meeting her eyes head-on in challenge as he absently rested a large hand on the girl's shoulder beside him.

Astrid leaned forward in her seat and pointed her eating knife at him. 'My father owes you a blood debt—I should be the one concerned about fair judgement here, not you!'

Especially as Viggo wanted to sell her off like a broodmare at the first opportunity.

'I will build a ship that beats yours in every way, and everyone will know I have won from merit rather than—'

'It will be fair.' Viggo interrupted their squabbling with a raised palm, and then scratched his red beard thoughtfully. 'My good friend King Olaf will be visiting us for the autumn blot. That should be enough time for you to each build a ship. He, not I, will determine the winner. They will become my undisputed master boat-builder. The loser…they will do whatever I *command*.'

The last word was heavily weighted.

Astrid glared at her father 'How so?'

'They will leave. Either in disgrace or as a bride… I think you know which one refers to you, my daughter.'

The Queen hissed something beneath her breath to Viggo, but he ignored her and stared his daughter down. 'Do you fear you will not win?' he goaded, and

after a long pause Astrid gave a sharp nod of agreement. What else could she do? Her father had deliberately set this whole situation up to undermine and
control her.

Viggo smiled, leaned back in his throne, and said
thoughtfully, 'We shall have three challenges to determine the speed, beauty, and strength of each ship.
You may have a team of ten builders each, four of
which will be from the current shipbuilders, the rest
thralls. That should be an equal share of the skilled
labour.'

Astrid was quick to respond. 'I want Revna and—'
Her words died as her father shook his head and held
up his clenched fist.

'They will be drawn by lots in three days' time.
I think it only fair that Ulrik be allowed some time
to acquaint himself with my kingdom before he be-
gins the challenge.' He fixed Astrid with a hard eye
as he lowered his hand. 'Not a single scratch will be
made on any tree or log until *after* the lots have been
drawn. All current work is to be stopped and put
away. Is that clear?'

Astrid nodded sourly. Her father was aware how
well she knew the forest, and of the many half-
finished carvings she had in her workshop. Still, it
wasn't as if she planned to cheat, and it annoyed her

that her father didn't trust her to behave honourably. Sometimes she felt as if he didn't know her at all.

Ulrik must have misunderstood, however, because he gave a disgusted huff. 'What are the challenges?'

Viggo thought for a moment before answering. 'Speed shall be determined in a race to the fjord's island rock and back. Strength will be judged on the number of barrels each ship can carry before dipping below the line. The final test will be made when King Olaf arrives. He will decide which figurehead is the most beautifully carved, without knowing the identity of who made it. Agreed?'

Astrid and Ulrik both nodded, but the animosity between them scorched the air.

'Ulrik can stay at the old master's workshop and home. I think it only fitting, as Ulrik has a daughter and you have a perfectly good chamber in the hall,' said Viggo with clear disapproval, which made Astrid suspect he already knew she lived at the beach most days.

Ulrik began to speak into his daughter's ear, as if reassuring her of something. It was strange to watch him behaving warmly to anyone. The girl looked at him with obvious devotion, and even refilled his cup with a proud smile. Afterwards he gave her a grateful pat on the arm filled with fatherly love.

But then again, even a snake could be kind to its own kin.

He and his daughter were both serpents, slithering into her home and usurping her rightful place! How dare he take what was not his? What he had not earned?

And why? Because she was a woman? The unfairness of it burned through her heart like a poison that would rot her from the inside out. She longed to throw an axe and split Ulrik's head in two, anything to rid her of this spiteful contest.

It was so obvious that her father did not want her to win. That he had brought an old friend home with him specifically to take her place.

It stung that her father would do such a thing. She knew that he did not approve of her work, and would have preferred her to be married as her older sisters were.

Every Jule or celebratory feast he filled the hall with potential suitors, but she had hoped after the *incident* last year that those days were finally behind her. That she could finally live in peace with her craft, without fear of a man's unwelcome touch or desire to control her.

It seemed not.

She glared at Ulrik with his sweet and obedient daughter. The kind of girl her father wished she was.

She imagined Ulrik thought he deserved her position more than she did, and thought these challenges unnecessary. No one would ever question his choices.

He had everything, and she had never hated a man more.

Chapter Two

'Is this to be our home?' asked Frida mournfully as she looked around at the cluttered workshop and longhouse.

Viggo had let them sleep last night in the hall, but they were eager to settle into their new home, and had sailed their fishing boat down to the shipyard after eating *dagmal*. However, the current state of the buildings was both confusing and disappointing.

'At least it's bigger than what we had before,' Frida added with a forced smile.

'True,' answered Ulrik as he stared at the mess in front of them with growing anger. Nothing about this new life had gone as expected.

Their new home had a large workshop at the front. It was basically a framed shelter with no walls that allowed in plenty of light, and had several work benches at its sides. Nothing unusual there. But next came the longhouse, and, from what little Ulrik could see, it had a central firepit, and several side-chambers divided by hazel screens.

It would have been a generous home if it weren't so full of timber.

Ulrik stepped carefully around the jumbled piles of discarded wood and tried to get a better look at the chamber beyond, but all he saw was more logs. It looked as if they'd been thrown inside without any care or consideration. One huge piece had even knocked over a table and bench, and now they lay broken amongst a sea of flotsam.

He nudged at a nearby pile with his foot and it tumbled down with a clatter. One piece had the carved outline of a horse's head on its surface. It was beautiful, and it oddly irritated him that such work would be so easily discarded, as if it were waste meant for the cesspit.

His fists clenched at his sides as he realised what his rival had done. Astrid had been ordered to put away all of her current work, and it appeared she had done so...by throwing every bit of it into his new home.

'Vixen!' he snapped.

Frida jumped beside him, startled by his rare display of emotion. 'I will clear it, Father—you must still go into the woods, as you planned.'

'That spoiled, petty, spiteful—'

Frida laid her hand gently on his elbow, a soothing balm on his hot temper. 'If we are going to win you will need to pick a good tree for the keel, will you not?'

'Yes, but...' He sighed miserably at the sight before him.

Sensing his doubt, Frida continued, 'And even though you cannot cut down any trees, you should at least use this time wisely before the lots are drawn. You will need the best timber you can find for your ship. So you must look for the best trees to fell, and the King did mention there is only one grove of strong oaks here, so you will need to find it.'

Everything she said was true, but how could he leave Frida to move this mountain of wood alone? 'I will at least move the bigger pieces before I go.'

Putting down their sacks by the entrance of the workshop, Ulrik began to drag out the larger pieces of logs, and pile them beside the side of his longhouse. Feeling particularly resentful, he threw the horse head on top of the neatly stacked crate of firewood. He hoped Astrid would see it, and regret her spitefulness.

Strangely, the cause of this chaos was nowhere to be seen—he would have thought she would have been here to gloat at least. But there was no one on the beach, and the smaller workshop beside them was silent. Presumably that was where Astrid would work, the tables and tools neatly ordered and clean. There was also a small forge, although it was currently empty, the ash in the furnace cold. The workers he had seen the previous day had disappeared like mist.

It must be part of Astrid's strategy to beat him in this contest. Last night she had left the feast early, her mouth full of bitterness, and he had been warned by several warriors to watch for her tricks. They said she should have been Loki's daughter, as the God of Mischief suited her far more than Viggo as a father. The warriors had laughingly recounted tales of her youth, and he had thought the jests sounded quite sweet and harmless.

He had not thought much of it—after all, he was not a man easily fooled. In fact, sometimes he wished there was a little more humour in his own life. He feared Frida was too serious for her age, and wished she would make time for youthful fun and games.

But this was not a simple jest, and he no longer thought Astrid quite so innocent. This was a deliberate attack, a way to delay him as he tried to settle Frida into their new home and prepare for the contest. Viggo had said that no tree or timber could be scratched until after the lots were drawn, but there was plenty of other work to do.

Especially as they were new arrivals, and unfamiliar with their surroundings. Sharpening tools, gathering supplies, and choosing the right trees to fell were all things he had planned to do in the time before the drawing of the lots. Something Astrid had realised and used against him. He now feared he would spend most of that precious time ensuring his new home was habitable.

But if he failed to prepare and lost the contest because of it, where would that leave Frida? He had no other skills, and his days as a warrior were firmly behind him due to his injury. This was the perfect opportunity, and if he had to unseat a spoilt princess to ensure his daughter's happiness then he would do so gladly. He only hoped the Norns of fate agreed, as otherwise he wasn't sure what they would do.

Maybe they should have stayed in Aalborg?

What if this venture came to nothing, and they were forced to leave?

What had possessed him to agree to this ridiculous challenge? Again, his temper had got the better of him, and rather than remain silent he had goaded the Princess into accepting the challenge. Maybe if he had stayed silent Viggo might have convinced her to step down quietly, and he wouldn't be desperately trying to prove his worth.

A dragging sound distracted him from his worries, and he saw Frida pulling out a piece of timber that was twice the size of her. She smiled brightly up at him, even as he saw the way her arms strained and her brow was beaded with sweat. 'See, Father,' she gasped, 'I can do it—you can go.'

His heart twisted sharply. It was the same optimistic smile Sigrid used to give whenever she was determined to do something challenging. Frida's mother had always been fearless, willing to try any task no matter how difficult. After his injury he had been weak and feeble for months, but she had taken on both their roles and duties without complaint. Nothing had daunted her, and it had cost her her life.

'I will do it!' Ulrik snapped, reaching for it.

Frida put down the wood with a thump, her tone surprisingly firm considering her age. 'Let me do it! I like it here, and I want to stay.'

He picked up the timber at her feet. 'This is too much for you to carry—you will end up hurting yourself.'

'I swear I will take care, and leave anything that I cannot carry alone. But I will do all that I can to make this a success. And I expect you to do the same…'

'You doubt me?'

'No, but you need to stop worrying about me, and focus on winning this challenge. We can always sleep in the boat if we have to; this…' she gestured at the mess around them '…does not matter. Your work does.'

Ulrik sucked in a shocked breath, but could find no fault with her reasoning. 'When did you become so wise?' he grumbled.

'I am no longer a child,' she said with a roll of her eyes. But she still looked like a child to him, and he suspected she always would.

Ulrik could only nod, a lump forming in his throat. 'Fine. But take your time, and no large pieces like this,' he warned, relaxing a little at her enthusiastic nod.

He dragged the wood to the side of the building and laid it down. Then he gathered a few supplies for his trip into the forest. 'I will be gone for most of the day, but I can help clear the rest before the evening meal. We won't need to sleep in the boat.'

'Yes, Father,' she answered dismissively as she continued to carry smaller pieces of wood outside and onto the wood pile.

When he hesitated, she waved him off, just as Sigrid might have done.

He walked away. His life had split in two. There was only the time before and after Sigrid's death. He had been left behind, helplessly watching as the time after began to stretch longer than the time before. Each day the distance between them grew, and the vibrant memories of her faded, until even his hold on them was weak.

Perhaps he should let go?

Frida could barely remember the face of her mother. Six winters had passed, and she was quickly turning into a woman. Life was constantly changing for both of them, and yet Ulrik felt as if he were still trapped in the waning light of the past.

He wanted to be a good father, to protect and provide for Frida with the strength of two hearts. But sometimes it did not feel as if he were truly living.

Chapter Three

Astrid sipped water from one of the mountain streams that led to the settlement far below. Up here it tasted as fresh and as cool as crisp apples. She sometimes wished she could live up here, alone and unbothered by her family's shadow. But that was a fanciful daydream—her father owned everything here, even the water in her cupped palms.

Rising up, she continued forward, knowing exactly where she needed to go to win the challenge. Most of the trees in the forest were pine, or ash, and although she would use many of those in the construction of her ship they were not what she wanted to see today.

Today she would be going to the grove of oaks. Rare this far north, these trees had been an odd sight for many years. Sometimes she wondered if they had been deliberately planted. If so, it must have been several generations ago, considering how mature they were.

Her father imported oak from the south usually, in exchange for the pines that were in high demand there. But he had said they were to take their materials from the forest, which meant the special grove was allowed, and Astrid had her sights firmly set on one specific tree.

A straight and mature oak, it would make the perfect material for the keel. She also wanted oak for her stem and stern, so would see what else was available. The stem and stern needed curved trees, as did the ship's ribs. But it was the keel that would determine the boat's eventual strength, length, and flexibility.

She would not take any chances with this build, and would use only the best oak. She might not be able to fell the tree now, but she would do all that she could in preparation.

After walking uphill for most of the morning she eventually reached the grove of oaks. They flowed up the steep hillside, heathers and ferns filling the ground beneath them. The best trees were at the top of the ridge, as they were unrestricted by light and pointed straight to the sky. While the ones further below curved up and out, as if stretching to kiss the sun. There was only one large, straight tree at the top of the ridge, the others around it being younger.

Perfect.

'*Heil*, Princess!' a deep voice rumbled beside her

and she jumped like a spooked horse. Ulrik smiled, as if taking a twisted pleasure in her fright. 'Surprised to see me? I expect you thought I would be spending all day clearing up your mess.'

She did not bother to deny it, only smirked. 'It was a jest! You really are very dull... You will not settle well here with such a dour disposition.'

'Moving your unfinished work into my new home is your idea of fun, *Princess?* I must admit, if that makes me dull, then I confess I must be. I would rather be that than reckless and spiteful. Although maybe I should thank you...for the *firewood*.'

She ignored the barb, although it struck a little too close to the bone, and she now regretted throwing in some of her half-finished pieces. 'New home? I doubt it. Prepare yourself for a disappointment. I will win fairly and with ease. Also, there is no need for titles— I am your equal.'

'My equal?' he snorted, as if the idea was ridiculous, and it sparked her anger, which only seemed to burn more fiercely with his next question. 'Why did you agree to this contest? Marriage would be a far better prospect for you.'

'You sound like my father,' she grumbled.

'Shipbuilding is hard labour, and leads to gnarled hands, bent backs and poor eyesight. Why would a young woman of high status ever want such a future—when she could live in luxury instead?'

'Because I enjoy it? Is that so hard to imagine? I am sure *your* reasons for shipbuilding are purely due to necessity and hardship. I, at least, love it for the art of the craft!'

'Why do you presume that?' he growled, shifting his stance, and crossing his arms over his chest.

'You were a warrior before, were you not? You have the physique of one, and Father said you took an axe for him...so I assumed you turned to boat-building when your injury...' she pointed to his bad leg, the one that caused him to limp in that swaggering way of his '...meant you could no longer fight, am I right?' she asked smugly, knowing she was right by the way his jaw clenched tightly.

However, his next words surprised her. 'Correct. Although carpentry is in my blood. My father was a boat-builder, and it was only natural I returned to it when my time in the shield wall came to an end. I probably have more experience than you... I bet you've barely even left this fjord.' She flinched and he smiled. 'How old are you anyway?'

'Were you not paying attention last night? My mother mentioned my age...you really should listen when the Queen speaks...' At his raised eyebrow and silent response, she grumbled, 'I have seen five and twenty winters.'

He ran a hand over the side of his head. 'That does explain it.'

'What?' she snapped.

His eyes hardened as he looked down at her. 'Your childish petulance, and spite.'

'How dare you?' she shouted.

'I thought we were equals, and could speak casually to one another—or is that only true if you like what you hear?' He raised an eyebrow and looked at her with those piercing eyes of his, stripping away all her pride with a single question.

Rallying her courage, she snapped, 'You think I should take insults without objection, just because you are my elder? How many winters have you seen, old man? Fifty?' In truth, she didn't believe him to be that much older than herself, but she delighted in the offence her words caused him.

Frowning darkly, he said, 'Five and thirty winters... I am not that old!'

She turned away to hide her smirk of amusement, but then was reminded of the purpose of her being here. She climbed up through the bracken, beating it away with a stick. To her surprise Ulrik kept pace with her, despite his leg. Maybe it was because he was so tall? His strides were much longer than hers.

She glanced at him and saw that he was looking at the same tree…

Her tree.

'Perfect, isn't it?' she asked mildly. 'But it will be mine. I am going to claim it first.'

He gave her a narrow-eyed look. 'Your father said there is to be no scratch made on any tree or log until after the lots are drawn.'

Triumphantly she pulled a long red ribbon from her bag. 'No scratch, but there are other ways to mark it.'

'You cannot claim it yet.'

'Why not?' And then with a laugh she ran forward, leaping up through the undergrowth with quick, sure feet.

When he eventually joined her at the top of the hill, she was still laughing to herself as she tied her ribbon to a low branch. 'I have the best tree. You may as well give up now!' she crowed. Her amusement died a little as she turned and saw his unaffected expression. It made her feel as childish as he had claimed her to be, and only fanned the flames of her resentment towards him. 'You accuse me of fighting unfairly, but you are the one with all the advantages! My father wants you to win—you could have been anyone, and he still would have brought you here. Have you no honour? Can you not see how wrong it is for you to come here? To steal my rightful place?

You said yourself my ships are well-built; there was no need for you to come here.'

'Did I?' he asked casually, looking around at the surrounding trees as if he was already bored of their conversation.

'You did! You said you only needed to complete minor repairs on *Dragon's Breath*. A boat is only as good as the quality of the wood used to make it, and I now have the best tree.'

He did not seem bothered by her victory, and wasn't even looking at her any more, but at a larger oak further to the side, balanced on the cliff's edge, half its roots exposed by an earlier landslide. It was much larger than her own and just as straight, but she had dismissed it as being in too awkward a position to fell safely.

Ulrik must have thought the same as his eyes swung back to hers, lazy and untroubled. 'You think a scrap of cloth makes it yours?'

'I think I will still beat you to the first cut,' she said with a dark smile. She had already proved she could outrun him.

Her glory was short-lived, however, as he only nodded. 'It matters not,' he said, limping to the trunk and tapping it with his hand.

Had he limped so heavily before the climb?

She tried to ignore the guilt that rose in her chest.

She did not want to pity him; she wanted to hate and loathe him with all her heart. That way she would not feel bad about sending him and his daughter away.

'It is a good choice, but I will not race you for it.'

She laughed at his bravado. 'Oh, the arrogance! You are so certain you will win?'

'As long as we play by the rules, I will.'

'Nobody plays fair,' she answered coldly. Her father certainly had not.

'I do,' he said firmly, and strangely she believed him. 'I expect you to do the same,' he added.

She raised a brow. 'Really? And what will you do if I do not?'

He shrugged. 'Nothing…but what will your father do?'

She swallowed the ball of resentment that had filled her throat. She knew what her father would do if he caught her breaking his rules—he would declare Ulrik the winner and gladly end the contest early. Which was why she would not cheat…a few tricks perhaps, but nothing that would give her father reason to end it.

'Well, I will go home now my work is done,' she said breezily. 'Good luck finding another tree. Maybe you should just accept your limitations…'

He scowled at her words and she realised her mistake too late. Her stomach churned with guilt. She had only been speaking about the tree, but did he think she was mocking his injury? 'With…the tree…' she added haltingly.

Why did her stupid mouth always make her seem the hot-headed fool?

In her hurry to move away from the awkward situation she tripped on a root. She would have landed flat on her face and tumbled down the hill if it weren't for the strength of Ulrik's arm that whipped out to grab her.

'You should be more careful—it is steep here,' he said coldly, his blue eyes hard as gems.

She jerked her arm from his and danced a few steps to the side, flustered by the sudden heat that now bathed her face and neck.

'Ha! I know this forest better than the back of my hand. I am perfectly—' The words were ripped from her throat as her boot slipped in the damp earth. She tried to regain her footing, but only seemed to slide backwards at greater speed. She grabbed at the nearest solid object and found Ulrik's tunic-covered shoulder. The worn material ripped as she twisted it in her fingers, and she would have taken half of his tunic with her down the mountainside if it weren't for his grabbing her upper arm.

There was a moment—suspended over the drop—when she thought all would be well. But then he hissed a curse of pain, his leg buckled beneath him, and the world tilted as they fell.

As if it was instinctual, Ulrik pulled her close and twisted his body as they fell, wrapping his arms around her head and shoulders as if to protect them. The fern-covered ground rushed up to meet them, and Ulrik grunted as he thudded down hard on his back, crunching bracken and twigs as he did so.

She winced at how much that must have hurt him, combined with the pain from his bad leg.

But then they began to roll with gathering speed, and she didn't have time to feel guilty. She tightened her hold on him and prayed for a quick death.

Like a pebble skipping across the water they tumbled, hitting rocks, snapping twigs and feeling every bump as they rolled over and over.

She yelped, all previous bravado forgotten, and he crushed her closer even as she heard his groans and hisses of pain. Eventually, Odin pitied them, because their tumbling began to slow. They bounced against a fallen tree, and the trunk rocked limply but still stopped them. Astrid sank into the rotten mulch, Ulrik on top of her, their breathing heavy and their limbs tangled in a lovers' embrace.

Astrid wanted to sink into the mud and never return.

Ulrik eased away from her, his hair a dishevelled

mess. Bracing a hand either side of her head, he lifted himself up onto his arms while he tried to regain his breath.

Dazed, she stared up at him, wondering idly for a moment if this was how he would look after love-making. Flushed and rattled, his eyes bright with exertion and surprise. He glanced up at the slope they had fallen down, and she found herself staring at the lines of his strong neck. Then down across a muscular chest, now revealed by his torn clothing.

Astrid had never been this close to a man's naked flesh before. When she had seen men wrestle or swim, she had sometimes admired their beauty, but this was overwhelming in comparison. That horrible incident with Bjarni did not even compare. No, not once had she felt like this. Hot and aching all at once.

Not only that, but he had also sacrificed himself to protect her, and it shook her to the core that a man she considered her his enemy would do such a thing.

Ulrik looked down at her, his head tilting as if he was examining her better. 'Are you well?'

His lips looked soft—she hadn't realised that before, but now, seeing them half-open as they were, she could almost imagine how tender they would feel against her own. Her heart thundered in her chest, and then she noticed his mouth twist upwards with a smirk.

'I agree with your father. It is past time you were wedded and bedded.'

'What?' she gasped, horror burning the butterflies in her stomach and turning them into ash.

'It must be, for you to be looking at me with lust in your eyes...or did you hit your head?' He asked the last question with a worried expression.

It must have been the fall. No wonder she felt light-headed and not herself. Embarrassment at being caught admiring him quickly erupted into anger.

'Are you out of your mind? You disgusting man! You are the one who has hit their head, not I! I would never consider you in that way, *never!*' She slapped at his chest with the palms of her hands, trying her best not to notice how solid his muscles were. 'Get off me! My father will cut off your hands for daring to touch me like this!'

She tried and failed to ignore the feel of his hot skin beneath her fingers, or the way his hips pressed down against hers a little as he struggled to raise himself up onto his knees.

Groaning, he moved to a sitting position beside her feet, and she saw raw pain shiver across his features for a moment before he gritted his teeth and looked away.

'Are *you* well?' she asked, guilt tempering her voice into a softer tone.

He laughed, and looked up at the fluffy clouds above them. 'I am alive, although Odin likes to tease me sometimes.'

Her heart broke at that statement, and she didn't know why.

'You should not say that—think of your daughter.'

His eyes snapped to hers and were filled with irritation. 'She is the only person I think of,' he snarled, bracing his arms against the fallen tree and heaving himself up onto his feet. Using mostly his remarkable upper body strength, rather than his knees, she noticed. It was impressive and she stared up at him a little shocked at how quickly he had risen.

Flustered, she stumbled to her feet, with less grace than he had shown, she realised, and slapped at her muddy clothes with irritation. 'Why did you bother saving me? If I had hurt myself badly or died, you could have had a clear win.'

He stared at her as if she were mad. 'I saved you *because* you are the King's daughter. You think I would live out this day if you were badly hurt or died whilst out in the woods with me?'

His answer was like a slap in the face, and she blinked rapidly, surprised by the pain. It had not been any real concern for her that had caused him to save her, she realised, and it stung her pride. Sometimes it felt as if she had no value in this world other than possessing her father's name.

Ulrik took out a piece of willow bark from a purse tied to his belt, and began to chew on it angrily as he limped forward a couple of steps as if to stretch his muscles.

'Will *you* be able to make it back?' she asked, gesturing to the herbal medicine he had taken, and trying her best not to look at his chest beneath the torn tunic. That sight led down a path of emotions which would only confuse and rattle her further.

He glared at her. 'I will be fine. My old wound only aches if I exert myself, or…if I tumble down a hill trying to save an ungrateful, spoiled princess!' He looked down at his torn tunic and cursed. 'You should be the one to give up this ridiculous contest, not I! Why would you want to be a boat-builder anyway? I would give anything for Frida to have even half of your opportunities.'

He grabbed her wrist and lifted it into the dappled light of the forest. She sucked in a sharp breath at the unexpected touch. His hand was firm, but the grip was not painful. In fact, it was warm and gentle, the pad of his thumb sliding down over her pulse and dipping into the hollow of her palm smoothly. Her thoughts scattered and she was helpless to do anything but watch the caress.

'You do not need to roughen these hands with hard labour. The right man would worship your body, and give you a life without burden.' His words were coaxing, as if he was trying to tempt her.

To her surprise it *did* sound appealing. But not in the way he might have imagined, because she could only imagine his hands on her, and not another's. She snatched her hand away as if scalded, which in a way was true. She stared at him, a little horrified that such an unkempt and odiously arrogant man could tempt her body to passion.

What was *wrong* with her? She had never been aroused before, not by *anyone*. Even with Bjarni she had only been tempted by his promises, never by his touch. But he had quickly proved that he would disappoint her in every way. Like her father, he couldn't be trusted. So, she had decided never to marry, because it only put her independence at risk.

After all, when she thought of marriage she was reminded of her mother's situation. Her endless days spent waiting and watching the seas for her husband's return, only to resent his power when he was home. Love could be a cruel tyrant, and she would bow to no master.

'I do not want or need a man!' she shouted, heat flooding her face as she tried to forget the burning touch of his hand. 'I do not want marriage, or a life without my craft. I would be bored and frustrated! Each day would be a punishment… I would feel like Loki, tied up and left all alone with only the slow drip of poison as my company. It would not be a happy life, it would be a horrible and miserable existence without beauty, purpose, or pride.'

Still breathless from her rant, she waited to see what he would say. But he only nodded, and began to walk ahead of her, his limp a little more pronounced than before, and once again her stomach twisted with guilt.

She called out to him, her heart hammering in her chest as she struggled to find the words. 'It is my dream! Why should I let you take it from me?'

He paused, and turned to look at her, his eyes surprisingly kind despite the tartness of his words. 'Dreams are easy for the daughter of a king. Find another, for I cannot.'

Chapter Four

Odin's teeth! The temptation to kiss her had been overwhelming.

Had he lost his mind on their tumble down the hillside? Even now, after walking for some time through the forest, he was still thinking through all the many disastrous outcomes such an act would have cost him.

His work, his home, his *sanity!* Everything could have been tossed overboard in that one breath-stealing moment. The memory of her expression as she lay beneath him would torment him for many days and nights to come. So beautiful and trusting. Her eyes filled with longing and desire, as if she might *actually* consider someone as low-born as him.

Which was laughable!

He had only caught her at a vulnerable moment, as she had caught him.

A chill slithered down his spine as he remembered

the terrifying moment when she had lost her footing. Bringing back painful memories as well as regrets.

Relief had flooded through him when he had stopped her falling, but then his damn leg had given way, and they had both tumbled down the hill helplessly. Still, it was better than her falling alone, as she might have cracked her head on a stone, or broken a bone—his own ribs felt a little bruised and he was much bigger than she was.

Needing time and distance, he slowed his pace so that she ended up walking a little ahead of him. Her back was caked from the top of her head to the heel of her boots in thick, sticky mud, broken leaves and sprigs of fern sticking out of her braid.

He imagined he looked even worse, and groaned when he saw who waited for them back at the workshops.

The King and Queen stood with Frida outside their new home. Everyone's eyes widened with horror when they saw them approach.

They must look wretched, like two children caught wrestling in the mud. Ulrik was certain he had looked better after a full day of battle than he did now.

Without a single doubt, Ulrik appeared the loser of their skirmish, what with his pronounced limp, torn clothing, and filthy body. His tunic, which had not been in the best condition to start with, was now no better than a rag hanging limply from his shoulders, exposing most of his chest and stomach.

Astrid's pace had slowed and they now walked side by side. He glanced at her, wondering if she feared her parents' disapproval. But if anything, her jaw had hardened and her nose was tilted high in a defiant gesture.

Why did she have to fight everything?

She was the kind of woman who would curse the stone that stubbed her toe, or scream at the wind that pulled her hair. Exhausting and wild, the kind a young warrior might seek to tame, but only receive a bloody nose for in the process.

Ulrik was wiser than that, surely?

Sucking in a deep breath, he prepared the words to defend himself against a rightly enraged father. He fully expected King Viggo to at least draw his sword, especially when he saw his bedraggled daughter, but to his surprise the King was glaring at Astrid and not him.

'Explain yourself and quickly!' shouted Viggo.

'Oh, Astrid! What did you do?' gasped her mother, and when Ulrik glanced at Astrid he saw a flicker of hurt cross her face before it was masked quickly by irritation.

'Nothing!'

He decided to intervene before anything more hurtful was said. 'Astrid was showing me the best trees in the forest, but we lost our footing and took a tumble. We are both well, and thankfully unharmed.'

Viggo's eyes did not soften, and he gestured towards Frida angrily. 'That is not *all* that she has done!'

Ulrik noticed the huge piles of wood at the side of their home, and he fought the urge to shout at his own daughter. 'I told you to wait for me. You should not have cleared all of it alone.'

'Oh!' came a weak gasp beside him, and then with more accusation, 'I thought you would be the one to do it, not her!'

He couldn't help it. He turned and glared at Astrid, opening his mouth to scold her, only to close it when he heard his daughter say, 'The King and his men helped me clear it!'

Viggo's hard gaze moved from Astrid to Frida and softened. 'Only the larger pieces. Your daughter is very hardworking, Ulrik, and insisted on preparing the house herself. Such a good and resourceful girl!'

Frida looked nervous at being the focus of so much attention, and Ulrik made his way over to her, leaning into the house to admire her work. Afterwards he rested a hand on her shoulder and gave her a proud smile. 'Did you do this, Frida? I am impressed.'

Frida nodded with a shy smile, too shy to say anything more in front of the King.

With another disapproving frown at Astrid—who ignored him—Viggo said, 'I only came here to make sure you were settled in well and remind you of the old oak grove in the forest. It is fortunate that I did, considering how much rubbish had been left in it!'

For a reason only the gods understood, Ulrik took pity on her. 'I saw the oak grove today; Astrid showed it to me.'

It took some of the wind out of Viggo's anger, and they spent a moment in idle talk, before the King and Queen returned to their hall. Without a word their muddy daughter followed behind them, stopping only for a moment as she passed him.

'You didn't have to say that,' she said, her expression still haughty despite all the dirt.

'I know.'

'I do not owe you anything.'

He chuckled. 'Of course not—why would you?'

She walked away, her back straight, and he was oddly glad that she had kept her pride.

Ulrik draped an arm around Frida's shoulders and gave them a squeeze. The sun was low in the sky and the fire beckoned. 'Show me what you have been up to, my darling girl.'

Frida reached around to hold him at the waist; she always knew when he was struggling. 'Does your leg pain you, Father? Should I boil some willow broth?'

'No. I think I have had too much willow bark as it is. I will rest it tonight.'

Frida helped him into their new home.

Home...already he could use that word to describe it. The scrubbed and polished furniture, the carefully embroidered blankets his wife had made and his daughter cherished. The flowers in a jug on the table, and the cauldron steaming above the fire.

'I thought we could eat here tonight, rather than at the hall,' Frida said quietly. 'The Queen gave me a basket of supplies, and I made a stew. I thought you would be tired after walking in the forest all day.'

Ulrik eased himself down on a chair and stretched out his cramping leg. 'That sounds perfect.' He leaned forward and peered into the cauldron, breathing in the fragrant herbs with a grateful sigh.

Frida smiled, and began moving around the room gathering bowls and spoons for their meal, while Ulrik tried to hide the throbbing pain with a smile that felt tight and brittle.

The ache would ease after a night of sleep, and he was grateful Frida had made them a meal so they didn't need to eat in the hall. In truth, he wasn't sure if he would have made it there tonight as it was.

He wondered how Astrid would fare tonight. If her father would punish her for her bad behaviour. He hoped not, although the spiteful woman deserved it.

Still, he had seen the way she flinched at her father's disapproval and he had pitied her.

The truth of what she had said in the forest struck his heart like an oar in the water, causing ripples of unease to shiver through him. He did not want to take her dream and purpose from her, not when she had already proved her worth.

It *was* unfair. He *was* usurping her place here. There was no reason to remove her as the master boat-builder—her work was good and she obviously loved it. Otherwise, why would she fight so strongly against his arrival?

But what was the alternative? To go back to Aalborg, remain working under his old master for a few scraps of silver—what future did that give Frida? Not her own home, or a dowry, or even a comfortable life.

No, he would not feel a moment's guilt about this contest.

So what if a spoilt princess had to give up on her trivial amusements so that he could build a life? The King approved of his place here; all he had to do was show that he deserved it.

Chapter Five

The large bathing tubs were the only luxury she missed when she lived away from the Great Hall. She had been meaning to carve one of her own for some time but kept forgetting, always finding some other more interesting piece to work on instead.

Tall wooden screens covered in cloth surrounded her, warding off the chill of the chamber beyond, and keeping the cleansing steam trapped within.

It might be her last chance to indulge in a long bath, what with many weeks of boat-building ahead of her.

She scrubbed her hair for the third time, using the juniper and moss soap her mother had given her, and then poured a jug of rinsing water over her head. She stood in the shallower of the two tubs. This one was used to clean off all the thick, caked mud from her hair and body before she could allow herself the more pleasurable soak in the deeper bath.

To her relief the rinsing water ran clear now, and

she wasted no time hopping from one tub and into the other.

Filled with fragrant herbs and hot water, the second bath soothed the bruises from her earlier fall with Ulrik.

Ulrik.

Even his name irritated her. It meant rich and powerful. But he was not rich and held no power over her, and yet he acted as if he did! As if he was so reasonable and justified in his actions. It drove her mad, not only because he was so self-righteous, but also because he made her question herself, in a way no other had.

She was used to the disapproval of others, had received it in varying amounts from her entire family most of her life. But she had stubbornly refused to let it affect her, until now.

Why was he any different?

Was it his daughter? She did feel bad about Frida, she was an adorable girl, and if Astrid had known she'd be left with the work of clearing the longhouse, then maybe she wouldn't have played that particular trick on him.

But he should not have left his daughter to clear it in the first place!

'Astrid!' called her mother from behind the screens, and she stifled another groan.

'Yes?'

'Would you like me to oil and comb your hair?'

The question was hesitant, and Astrid almost gave an immediate *no*, but then she remembered she wanted to live at the workshops during the build, and she would need her mother's support if she was to be granted permission. 'Yes, please. Come in!'

The Queen entered wearing only her shift. 'The steam will ruin my gown,' she explained, a comb and clay bottle of precious hair oil in her hands.

Taking a nearby stool, she sat behind Astrid and began to comb out her hair gently. 'Your father says Ulrik is talented in carving as well as design. So do not be complacent with the figurehead. It must be bold, but also intricate.'

'It will be my best work,' Astrid reassured her, before leaning forward and resting her arms on her knees, so that her mother could reach the tangled ends of her hair. 'It will give all those who see it nightmares!'

Her mother chuckled softly. 'Good. If you win the test of beauty, then you need only choose to build your ship for speed or cargo. Have you decided which will suit your tree better?' Astrid had told her mother she would be going to the oak grove to choose her tree.

'Speed.'

The comb hesitated mid-movement. 'Your ships

have been better with load in the past. Do not take your father's words to heart.'

'If that is the only criticism of my ships then I shall prove him wrong, and I will win all three challenges So, there is no doubt in my skill.'

Her mother's quick fingers returned to work, braiding her hair, and dropping it over the lip of the bath. 'There was never any doubt in your skill...no matter what your father says.'

Astrid sighed, leaning back against the wooden tub's high back. She turned a little to see her mother better. 'Why have you always been so understanding?'

Her mother busied herself with picking up the filthy clothes from the floor, and dropping them in a basket. 'It makes you happy.'

Astrid felt a twinge of guilt—she had meant to put them there, but had been too eager to shed them and get clean. Now she felt like a naughty child again. 'But you must wish I was more like my sisters...that I would marry, as Father wants me to.'

Her mother shook her head. 'I want you to be happy. I may not always understand the paths you choose, but I have always known you would not be satisfied with marriage in the same way as your sisters. You are too...wild.' Her mother smiled softly.

Astrid frowned, lazily circling the cooling water

with her hand. 'Will you speak to Father? Explain how I can never marry?'

'Your father does not listen to me. He never has…' The words were bitter and resentful, but also filled with hurt.

Astrid had heard many of her parents' long and exhausting arguments, which usually ended in Viggo leaving on another voyage. Neither of them resolved the trouble between them, and when he returned they seemed to pick up their disagreement as if he had never left.

It was unbearable to watch, and the main reason why she had ended up learning shipbuilding from Revna and her husband. It had been a welcome respite from the squabbles of her family. Theirs had been such a different relationship to her parents'. One built on mutual love and respect. As she had grown up she had realised how rare such a peaceful life was.

Astrid was not built for such a life. Her temperament was too…much. Fiery and stubborn, she was a strange combination of her parents' greatest faults. Marriage seemed to fit some women like a well-made glove. Women like her sisters, who were willing to bend to the will of another so they could live a pampered life, or women like Revna who were patient and kind…and easy to love.

Astrid was not an easy person to live with, and her

parents reminded her of that daily. She was odd, reckless, and unforgiving. She could not understand how her mother, who was so strong in many ways, could so easily do as her husband wished.

'You are still his Queen!' Astrid reminded her desperately. 'You rule this land in his absence. In fact, you have ruled it for far longer than him, considering how often he is away.' It always irritated Astrid that her freedoms were heavily curbed in her father's presence.

Her mother looked towards her then, her spine straightening with pride as well as rancour. 'I am Queen in his absence, and I was Queen of this land before we were even married. But he is still the ruler here, never forget that.'

'I know.' Astrid sighed wearily, repeating what she had heard over and over. 'Your marriage to Viggo brought peace to Viken. By winning your hand, he ensured prosperity for all.'

It was a tale her father had told many times. How their marriage had united two kingdoms. Often, he used it to remind Astrid about the place of women in society. In his words, they were all treasures, and with their beauty they could buy peace and happiness for all by uniting families.

Her mother surprised her with a sharp look. 'He won my hand with false words and promises of love.

But I do not regret my decision. For all his faults, he gave me my children, and my people are happier because of our alliance.'

Astrid sighed, and wished she could dunk herself beneath the water. It made her miserable that her mother would still openly side with her father. In private she may agree with her, but what use was that?

Inga walked towards her, and gave her a firm look. 'All I want is for you to be happy. If that means building ships, then build your ships. Prove to him that we women are not so easily bent and broken to men's will.'

'I will try…' Astrid said weakly, but the task felt insurmountable. How could she ever win against her father?

'I am sure you will succeed. You are far stronger than I ever was, and certainly braver. Unlike me, you will be ruthless in fighting for what you want…'

It was as if her mother had revealed a secret part of her soul, and just as quickly it was hidden beneath dignity and grace. As her mother lifted the cloth to leave, she said, 'Astrid, I do not want you to be anything but what you are…my daughter.'

At the evening meal, Astrid decided to broach the subject of where she would be living. Her father seemed in a good mood, and her mother's earlier words had given her some confidence. But rather than approach it directly she decided to circle around it until the opportunity arose.

'Does Ulrik not have a wife?' she asked lightly.

Her father sat back in his chair with a sigh and wistful eyes. Astrid could tell he was about to go into one of his long stories. 'Yes, he did. I remember him mooning over her before battle—I was worried it would make him careless. But it did not affect his courage. He struck out with as much fire as any young man wishing to win glory for himself. When my shield split, he covered me with his, and it cost him his leg. I remember him being carried to the healer after it was over, and he was not afraid. He only feared what would become of his wife. He loved her deeply, as if she were the sun in the sky, and the earth beneath his feet.'

Inga's smile could have cut through stone. 'How *sweet*… Such love is rare. Many profess to possess it, but most fail to truly feel it.'

Her father fell silent, and began to push his food around with his knife with little enthusiasm.

What would be better? Astrid wondered. To experience true love, but only for a short time, or never to experience it at all?

'His girl is an impressive homemaker…from what I saw…' said Astrid thoughtfully. Viggo seemed to approve of this change in conversation, and he began to speak loudly with much gesturing.

'Frida is a very good daughter. Obedient, kind, and hardworking. She had that longhouse clean and welcoming in the blink of an eye!'

Astrid ignored the arrows sent her way. It was the reaction she'd wanted from her father after all. 'So, he will be well looked after by her.'

'Very well looked after! Even though she be young, she is a capable girl! If only—'

Astrid interrupted him quickly, 'Well, then, it is only fair I stay close by my workshops. The journey back and forth will use up precious time that I could use carving.'

Her mother flinched. 'You want to live down there? When you have a perfectly good bed here?'

'I must use all daylight available to me.'

Realising his mistake, her father grumbled. 'It is hardly a long voyage walking up and down the beach.'

'It will still use up precious time. I will stay with Revna in the smaller longhouse—she is coming from her daughter's farm in two days, when the lots are drawn. It is only fair that I have equal time on my ship as Ulrik has on his.'

Both her parents looked as if they had swallowed a fly.

Inga was the first to recover. 'Stay here at least

until the drawing of the lots. I will organise some furniture and supplies for you,' she said quietly, and when Viggo tried to argue her mother shook her head firmly. 'It is only fair.'

Astrid felt a twinge of guilt knowing that her mother would miss her terribly. Even though they did not enjoy the same things, or understand each other well, there had always been a solidarity between them. It had always been *them* against Viggo.

Yes, it would be better never to taste true love, or its inevitable disappointment.

Her mother had, and she was the loneliest person Astrid knew.

The next two days were painful.

News of her father's return had spread throughout the land. This had brought her two elder sisters to their door, as well as their husbands. Every moment was deliberately dedicated to ensuring she knew all the virtues of marriage, and it was exhausting.

Tonight at *nattmal* felt particularly dreadful. It was the night before the drawing of the lots and her stomach was filled with butterflies. She felt as if she was being harassed by relentless merchants while trapped in a market. Her sisters chattered constantly either side of her, selling her a life she had no interest in buying. But from the regular nods of approval her father gave Bodil and Liv, she was certain they had been ordered to do so.

It wasn't that she didn't believe her sisters to be happy in their marriages, only that she knew from experience how different she was to either of them. Growing up, her sisters had always dreamed of a husband and children, and the only challenge they enjoyed was boasting to each other about who had 'won' the better man, while Astrid thought both her brother-in-laws rather dull, and did not envy her sisters' matches in the slightest.

Somehow it was all made worse by Ulrik and Frida's presence. They sat quietly at an end table, Frida's eyes bright with excitement, obviously thrilled to be taking part in such a grand feast, while Ulrik looked as happy to be there as she felt. She had not seen him since their fall in the forest, and she had been worried by the quantity of willow he had eaten on the way back. He must have been in a lot of pain, and she had been the cause. She idly wondered if he now hated her, and then tried to ignore how uncomfortable that made her feel.

It still surprised her that despite his suffering he had not taken the opportunity to humiliate her in front of her family. She would not have done the same, and it shamed her a little to know it.

'It is so nice to be in charge of your own household,'

said Bodil, smiling lovingly at her husband, Jarl Leif, who was currently wrestling with Jarl Kalf, Liv's husband. The benches had been cleared to allow for such contests of strength.

Liv leaned forward with a teasing smile. 'I believe my Kalf will win this time, Bodil.'

Bodil laughed. 'Is that so? I will bet my whalebone comb that he will not.'

Liv grinned. 'And I will bet my…' she thought for a moment '…my bronze turtle brooches he will!'

Bodil's eyes lit up, and she shouted out to her husband, 'Defeat him, Leif! I will reward you well for it!'

Leif glanced their way and grinned at his Bodil slyly. 'Is that a promise?'

Bodil giggled. 'I swear it!'

With a mighty roar Leif grabbed Kalf and threw him down, claiming victory over the match. Bodil jumped up and cheered. Then turned to laugh at her sister's horrified face.

Liv smacked her sister's arm sharply. 'Fine! Besides, *my* husband can buy me another pair easily! Our trading settlement is very prosperous after all. I am so fortunate to have such a rich husband.'

Bodil shrugged, returning to her seat. 'Good, then my husband can win more treasures from you at our next meeting.'

Liv glared back at her as if she wished to pluck out her eyes.

Astrid sipped her ale in silence, unconcerned by her sisters' bickering. She knew there was no real animosity between them. They were as quick to defend as they were to scold one another.

They had always been this way, constantly competing and squabbling. Astrid preferred not to get involved in their arguments, as they were more likely to turn on her than anything else.

She had never felt welcome in their company.

Perhaps it was because they were so close in age, whilst there was more of a gap between them and Astrid. Her brother had come after them—the long-awaited heir, and she had been more of an after-thought, too young to play with the elder girls, and only allowed to play with her brother for a short time, before their father took charge of his training. It had led to a lonely childhood, it was no wonder that she had sought companionship with Revna and her family.

'Tell me, daughters,' said Viggo loudly, interrupting Astrid's thoughts. 'Are you happy with the fine men I found for you?'

Bodil and Liv both nodded eagerly like obedient hounds performing tricks for their master.

'And you enjoy being the mistress of your own household?'

Again the women nodded, their red hair shining in the golden light of the hall. Astrid noticed Ulrik looking at them with interest, and she felt like a dead fish in comparison to their bright beauty.

'I have such talented and pretty daughters. Bodil is an expert at brewing delicious ale, and Liv makes the finest cloth,' said Viggo to no one in particular, although his daughters preened at his compliments. It was not lost on Astrid that her sister's crafts were only seen as acceptable because they were traditionally feminine pursuits. 'Have you heard about the boat-building challenge?'

Bodil and Liv nodded again.

'Well, we will need two sails for these ships. Can you provide them, Liv? They must be the same in every way…to ensure a fair contest.'

'Yes, Father.' Liv nodded, although she glanced at her husband with concern in her eyes. A single sail was time-consuming to produce, and cost a fortune in materials, let alone two.

'I will help provide the wool,' reassured Viggo, and Liv's shoulders relaxed. 'Of course. We will need them for the midsummer festival. Even though King Olaf will judge the boats at the autumn blot, it will be important that they are rigged well before. What better time than at the most anticipated celebration of the year? Bodil, can you make ale for the celebrations? We will need plenty for both the midsummer and autumn festivities.'

Bodil nodded, but she was quick to point out, 'I will need help with the grain, Father.'

Viggo smiled and nodded. 'Of course, it will be nice to have all my children here for both celebrations. It will be like old times...' Inga blinked with surprise and frowned with displeasure at his claim. Astrid herself could remember only one midsummer when her father had been present. 'In fact,' continued Viggo, 'we should invite all of my Jarls to join with us... Festivals are a great time to encourage and build alliances.'

Astrid's eyes immediately rolled at her father's obvious plan. Her mother gave her a sympathetic look, but they both knew they could say nothing about it. No doubt the midsummer festival would be when her father would gather, and then decide on, the best potential suitors for her, inviting only the best bulls to return for the autumn blot—just in time, if she lost, to hand her over to one of them before the winter set in.

Viggo never wasted an opportunity, and he obviously thought her incapable of winning the contest. It should not hurt or come as a surprise to Astrid that her father doubted her, but it did.

She threw back the contents of her horn and then reached for the jug of mead to refill it. That was when she caught Ulrik staring at her from across the room, and to her horror there was sympathy in his eyes.

How dare he pity her?

She gave him a murderous glare, daring him to hold her gaze. Finally, those piercing blue eyes of his moved away, and she smiled to herself in triumph. It was her first win, and she would cherish it.

Chapter Six

Ulrik eyed the fifteen men and five women who stood in front of the two workshops waiting for the lots to be drawn. Twelve were thralls from the hall, all strong labourers, but not skilled in the art of boat-building. They would help run the camp, and do the easier tasks such as splitting and carrying wood. They were the hard labour—without them there would be no chance of building two ships in time for the autumn blot.

The eight skilled workers were Bo, Knud, Frode, Gorm, Sten, Odger, Arne, and Revna—the name Astrid had immediately asked for. Curious as to why the only woman of the skilled workers would be her first choice, he had asked around about Revna. She was the previous boat-builder's wife, and had helped train Astrid.

According to the people he had spoken with at *natt-mal*, Revna was a close friend to Astrid—a second mother, some said, although quietly. Only recently had she taken to living at her daughter's farm, ever since her first grandchild had been born. Which was why he had not met her until now.

The woman looked to have seen at least ten more winters than himself. She had long silver hair woven with several dark ribbons and little wooden carvings that clicked lightly as she moved. She was short and stout, with a large bust and strong legs. There was a calm confidence in her manner, but also a soft motherliness too.

Revna was the first person Astrid greeted when she arrived at the workshops, rushing over from the King and Queen to embrace the older woman in a crushing hug. 'How is your daughter, and the new grandchild? I heard she had a boy—have they chosen a name?' she asked in a rush.

Revna smiled warmly, and patted Astrid's shoulder as if to calm her. Before answering Astrid's questions, she gave a respectful tilt of her head to the King and Queen. 'Yes, she has had a fine boy, and they have named him Garold.'

'Oh!' gasped Astrid with delight. 'How lovely! Maybe he will grow to be a master builder like his namesake?'

'Perhaps…although I think him better suited for battle if his war cry is anything to go by!' Revna rubbed at one of her ears as if it were sore, and Astrid gave a shout of laughter. Ulrik had never seen her laugh like that before, so openly and without an ounce of spite or bitterness. It was…confusing.

It was as if he were watching a different woman, a happier one. The kind that got watery-eyed over baby names, who laughed and hugged her friends as if the difference in their social standing meant nothing.

He could tell the pair had lived and worked side by side for many years. It was interesting that Revna had never questioned Astrid's place as master. The people he had spoken to said she had never even tried to claim the position for herself.

Which did not surprise him.

Who would dare question the will of a princess? Except, no one here acted as if she was a princess.

They all gave her warm smiles, and friendly waves as she greeted them. It reminded him of the King's nature, and when he looked to him, he saw the man was undisturbed by the familiarity, and was already busy with the task of the morning.

Viggo held out a sack and shook it at him. 'Draw your first name.'

An oppressive silence descended over the group. Stepping forward, Ulrik placed his hand inside the bag and drew the first stick that touched his fingers.

Astrid had turned to face him, her mouth slightly open as if her breath had caught in her throat.

Turning the stick in his hand, he read the name painted in runes along it. 'Revna.'

Astrid strode towards him, with fire in her eyes and a hiss on her lips. 'Could you not wait for me to join you at least?'

'Revna, go and stand at Ulrik's workshop,' ordered Viggo, and the woman did as he asked.

'Why did he get to choose first?' Astrid's face was flushed as she glared at her father accusingly.

'Why does it matter? We are still drawing lots,' Viggo replied coldly.

Without hesitation Ulrik handed the stick to Astrid. 'Have Revna, then. But you cannot pick and choose the rest, Princess. You must accept the will of the gods.'

He could tell he had shocked Astrid, because she stared at his outstretched hand for a long time without speaking, as if afraid to accept his offer.

Viggo cursed. 'How is that accepting fate? It was meant to be a fair selection.'

'Maybe he would rather no women were in his team?' Astrid asked suspiciously, and when he said nothing she snatched the stick from his hand. 'Well, then, I will not say no, even if you are making a terrible mistake.'

Viggo's scowl swung between them with equal weight, but eventually he nodded and Revna quietly moved to stand outside Astrid's workshop instead. He shook the bag once more at Ulrik. The look he gave him was so severe that Ulrik knew without a doubt that if he did not accept the next choice, Viggo would throw both the bag and Ulrik straight into the sea.

Ulrik was not worried—he had only been willing to concede one name. Reaching in, he picked out another stick. This time it had Bo's name scrawled across it.

He breathed a sigh of relief. Bo was a huge bear of a man, and the settlement's blacksmith by trade. He had spent the last few days making hundreds of nails for both ships, so Ulrik had already witnessed what he was capable of, and he would need the man's strength if his leg caused problems for him later.

It had plagued him for the last couple of days. So much so that he had been forced to rest it for nearly two days. Still, it had allowed him to get to know the builders—all except Revna—and he felt confident he could work with any of them. But he was still pleased to have Bo on his team.

They took it in turns to pull the remaining names from the bag, and then divided the unskilled workers equally. Viggo had ordered a few makeshift buildings and tents to be raised in the last two days, and the workshops now looked like a little village, providing enough accommodation and supplies to last them the rest of spring and into autumn.

In the end Ulrik's skilled team consisted of Bo, Odger, Arne, and Frode. While Astrid had Revna, Knud, Gorm and Sten.

'I wish you all good luck in this contest…may fortune favour…' Viggo paused, as Astrid had gathered her team around her, and was speaking quietly with them '…the victor.'

As if she were waiting for that final word, Astrid and her team suddenly charged off at a sprint towards the forest, as if the ground were on fire beneath their feet.

Viggo turned to Ulrik, his expression darkening further when he saw how unconcerned he was by their sudden departure. 'Go, then! Do not be afraid just because she is my daughter!'

'I am not,' Ulrik replied, unable to help smiling as he noticed the only one who hadn't run was Revna, she was currently speaking with the Queen with warmth and affection as if they were old friends.

Viggo was not finished in his reprimand. 'During this contest, Astrid will no longer be a princess. She is your challenger, and you are my *champion*. I expect you to win!'

Ulrik nodded, strangely irritated by Viggo's words. 'I will.'

'Then should you not be on your way?' he snapped, pointing towards the already distant figures of Astrid's team. 'You do not want her to get ahead of you—she will be going straight to the grove of oaks!'

Ulrik shook his head. 'There is no rush. I know which tree Astrid favours and I am not interested in it. The one I want will be awkward to fell and I must prepare for it.'

'So much effort for one tree? I thought it took many trees to build a ship; why take such care with one?'

Ulrik noticed the Queen had left, and Revna was watching him curiously. 'It does. But you must pay particular attention to the tree used for the keel. It must be naturally straight.'

Revna smiled, either with amusement or admiration, he couldn't be certain which, then she walked away towards the forest, her pace slow and thoughtful.

Viggo scrubbed a hand down his face as if already exhausted by the day's events. 'I shall trust you know what you are doing. But do not disappoint me in this. I chose you not only because you saved my life, but because I hoped you had the skill to beat her.'

Viggo stared at him with a look that reminded him of one of Astrid's glares, and he found it a little unsettling. Astrid was beautiful, and took after her mother's fine features, but her manner and bearing was that of a King.

'I will not fail in this challenge. I am determined to make a home here for Frida, and, though it pains me to remove a skilled craftswoman from her position, I will do so to ensure my own family's happiness.' The words tasted strange on his tongue, despite the many times he had repeated them to himself.

It seemed to appease Viggo, however, and the King began to turn away. Unable to help himself, Ulrik asked, 'Why do you want Astrid to lose? Have you a match already planned for her?'

Viggo scratched his beard thoughtfully, his eyes fixed on the horizon. 'No, but there is one man I would like for her, one that even Astrid cannot refuse. It is time she stopped embarrassing me with her reckless ways and learned her place. Farewell, Ulrik, and let me know if you need anything.'

Ulrik nodded and watched as Viggo walked back towards his hall. The King's words should have reassured him that his victory was inevitable. But instead, it tightened an already uncomfortable knot deep in his gut.

Frida caught his eye; she was giggling uncontrollably as she tried to herd an errant chicken back into its pen. He smiled, but it felt tight. That was when he realised why he pitied Astrid, and why her genuine laugh had startled him.

As a father, Ulrik wanted nothing more than to see his daughter living a happy life. But Astrid could never do that, as her father did not want her to be happy—he wanted her to be obedient, and to follow the path of a princess.

It must be hard for Astrid to live with her father's constant disapproval. An unexpected pity for his rival bloomed in his heart. But he squashed it like a bug.

Life was unfair.

He had to remember that.

Chapter Seven

By the time Ulrik arrived at the grove Astrid had felled her tree and was already preparing to have it taken down to the beach. The useful branches had already been cut, and now she and her team were stripping it of what remained.

Had Ulrik accepted that she would win this race?

It should be a relief, but it sparked a twisted resentment within her. A part of her, a very *small* part, had relished the challenge. Now she had worked herself up into an unnecessary frenzy over a man who didn't seem to even care!

She had run to reach her tree first...*run!* What an idiot she must have seemed when he had no intention of racing after her. It had not been a dignified start to the challenge, and she was more than a little embarrassed by her childish behaviour.

Did he not care that he had lost the best tree?

It made her suspicious. Had Ulrik found a better

tree somewhere else? Except there were no similar oaks between here and the workshops. According to her team, Ulrik had not left the beach except to visit the hall since their ill-fated trip in the woods. Knud had even mentioned that he seemed particularly sore after their fall, keeping to his longhouse for a couple of days. Which had *almost* made her feel sorry for him.

Or did he have another plan?

Would he go to her father and report that she had unfairly claimed the best tree before the official start of the competition? Would her father arrive and demand she hand it over to Ulrik? After all the work that had gone into felling it? Her unease grew with every passing moment.

When Ulrik did eventually arrive in the glade with his men, it felt as if a milling stone had been taken off her shoulders.

Her father was not with him, thank Odin!

Bo was carrying a huge wooden frame on his back. It looked as if several planks had been bound together with rope, and then rolled up like a bunch of kindling. Curious, she stopped what she was doing and watched them amble up the hill towards her.

'The best tree is taken!' she called out, and tried to ignore the strange look Revna gave her from across the trunk.

Yes, she sounded petty.

But it was impossible to stop herself. Ulrik was an itch she couldn't help but scratch.

He paused beside her, his big, hairy body filling the space, and she was almost tempted to take a step back when the earthy scent of his musk hit her nose.

'If you say so,' he replied in an infuriatingly bored tone, but there was a spark of mischief in those bright blue eyes that called to her wicked heart.

Astrid laughed, looking to Revna for agreement, but she seemed to be avoiding her gaze at that precise moment. 'What other possible tree is there?'

He leaned down towards her slowly, as if he was about to tell her a secret, and she found herself holding her breath in anticipation as he murmured, 'That one.'

Ulrik pointed to the majestic oak which stood in defiance beside the cliff edge. It was a beautiful tree, but it had almost been lost the previous year when a landslide had nearly taken it over the cliff. Some of the roots were even exposed, reaching out gnarled fingers to the sea below, as if tempting fate.

'But...' She stared at the oak, and then at Ulrik, who to her utter surprise grinned. She had never seen such a smile from him before, and it knocked the breath from her body. He always seemed so dour and serious. It was a rare insight into the playful man beneath, seeing the sharp whiteness of his teeth, and the twinkle of his eyes. It *fascinated* her, and she found herself staring into his face for far too long.

'It is strong, and tall. An excellent choice for my keel,' he explained with a gruff clearing of his throat, and to her dismay the smile was gone.

Shaking her head as if to clear her thoughts, she cried, 'But…you will never be able to fell it! There is nowhere to stand! And if you cut it from this side it will drop into the water, and then it will certainly break against the rocks, making it useless for anything more than planks at best!' She felt breathless by the end of her rant, and was uncomfortably aware of how close they still were…had she stepped even closer?

A sly smile that felt colder than the one before cut through his thick beard as he looked down at her. 'You lack imagination, *Princess*.'

Why, when he called her Princess, did it feel as if it gripped her by the throat?

As if he were telling her that there was still so much for her to learn, and not only about tree-felling.

Heat burned up her neck and face, and she was grateful when Revna called to her, the rope she had thrown landing on the trunk next to her with a slap. Distracted by the task at hand, she began to knot it, relieved when his shadow slipped away.

'You will want this moved before dusk. Do not

concern yourself with the work of others. It will only drive doubt into your heart,' reminded Revna sagely and Astrid nodded. Self-doubt was a beast she had spent many years trying to tame. So she busied herself removing branches, and sectioning the trunk.

However, unable to help herself, she occasionally found her eyes shifting to Ulrik and his work. The planks had been unrolled to form a platform which was now being tied and weighted around the base of his tree, like a fanned-out skirt.

'He is mad!' she grumbled to herself.

Revna gave her a curious look. 'It is unusual, but quite clever really. There is no other oak that would make an excellent keel—except this one, of course,' she said, patting the broad trunk in front of her affectionately. They had waited many years to use this tree, and although Astrid was pleased to have it, the burden of using it wisely made her nervous.

Watching Ulrik's ridiculous strategy unfold did not help!

'But…it is dangerous, and he is more likely to kill someone than be able to fell it safely!'

Revna smiled. 'Possibly, or he might get himself an equal match for your keel…without having to run for it.'

Astrid cut off a branch with one sharp swing, and then gestured at Revna with the head of her axe.

'Would you have preferred being in his team? I can always send you back!'

At her harsh words, Revna gave a wheezing chuckle. 'I still do not understand why you insisted on me taking part. It is not as if I can teach you anything—you learned all you needed from Garold years ago.'

Astrid lowered her axe. 'I need you. Who else will support and guide me?'

Revna's smile turned bittersweet and she nodded. 'I will always do that. But it is a shame you never listen.'

Astrid laughed, ignoring her friend's jab. The day's work progressed well from then on, although she deliberately kept her back towards Ulrik and his men to avoid becoming distracted by their madness.

However, the curiosity gnawed at her like a dog with a bone, and as midday came and went she wondered if his tree would ever be felled.

She breathed a sigh of relief once her own trunk was bare of its branches. It had all gone as she had hoped. While the thralls transported it safely to the beach, she could focus on choosing the curved trees she would need for her ribs, stem and stern.

But, instead of focusing on the next task, Astrid finally gave in to temptation, and asked Revna, 'Is he even ready to fell it yet?'

She pretended to be inspecting the trees opposite

while she waited for Revna's reply. She did not need to explain who *he* was, because Revna immediately looked over her shoulder to assess Ulrik and his men.

'Well, he has the others felling the smaller trees around it and laying the logs horizontally. Perhaps he hopes to roll it down to a safer position once it is felled?'

Astrid gave a nonchalant shrug, but she had to admit it was a good idea. It would certainly be safer, and the felled trees would not go to waste.

'And now,' Revna said with a shocked laugh, 'Ulrik is jumping up and down on his platform, testing its strength.'

'What?' Astrid gasped and spun on her heel. Revna spoke true, the madman was jumping up and down on a rickety wooden platform that jutted out into the air.

She stumbled forward, not quite sure what she planned to do, but unable to stand by as Ulrik risked his life in such a ridiculous way. She was halfway to him when her heart slowed a little—it went from frantic, to merely a skittish beat. A rope was wrapped around him, its end anchored to another tree. He had taken one precaution at least.

'Are you sure this is safe?' she called out.

'Why are you so concerned?' he called back, looking more elated and cheerful than she had ever seen him before.

Did he truly long for death?

'I would not wish to win only because my rival fell stupidly from a cliff on the very first day of the challenge!' she snapped back, her words bitter in her mouth. 'It would be a waste.'

'I am surprised you care that much about me.'

'Of the trees! It would be a waste of the trees...' she muttered.

Ulrik laughed, hiking his great axe into position, and resting it for a moment on the breadth of his broad shoulder. There was something very disconcerting about his smile, so wide and sharp it seemed to illuminate his dark-bearded face, which otherwise was so overgrown and shadowed. 'I am making the best of my limitations...as you have advised, Princess.'

Astrid tried to ignore the looks of the men and Revna around her. These were her friends, and she felt a prickle of shame claw up her face and neck at his censure in front of them. Their eyes of judgement pierced through her bravado to the scared girl beneath.

Why did he make her feel like a spiteful child?

Because you have acted like one? Came a guilty voice from the depths.

'Help them clear the path. Those two trees should go too, just to be safe,' said Astrid, and her people went to work on the trees she had pointed out.

'You want to help me?' called out Ulrik with a bewildered expression.

'I will use the timber from those,' she replied coolly, but in truth the wood would only be useful for minor rib and hull pieces. Still, this was as generous as she was willing to be, and the only kind of apology he would receive from her.

A loud, cracking thud filled the air, followed by the shiver of leaves. Ulrik had made the first cut. Bo's axe quickly followed from the other side of the trunk, positioned lower to encourage its fall on the grove side rather than on Ulrik's.

Ulrik had a pile of wedges at his feet, which would also be used to encourage the direction of the tree's fall. To distract herself, she tested the rope that held him. The knot seemed sturdy enough, and so she watched the crown of foliage as it shook and trembled with each beat from the axes below.

Bo, a blacksmith who had worked closely with her for many years, was an exceptionally strong man, but Ulrik matched him with each blow. Thick beats of the axes mingled with the straining breaths of the two men at work. Soon their hard labour began to pay off, and Bo moved aside so that Ulrik could rain death blows upon the trunk. The tree began to lean, and the creak of timber and the shudder of leaves signalled its final breaths.

But then there was another crack, followed by several more. 'Ulrik!' shouted Astrid, having no time to say anything more in warning.

Ulrik's eyes flew upwards, and widened as he saw a large branch slam through the canopy, breaking branches like twigs as it dropped towards him.

Astrid did not hesitate—she grabbed the rope beside her as Ulrik leapt off the platform, only moments before the thick branch smashed through the platform like kindling. The rope burned through her hands as Ulrik's weight pulled it taut. Thankfully, the knot held firm, and in truth he did not need her help, but she would never have forgiven herself if it had snapped and she had not at least tried to hold on.

Then with a deafening crash the rest of the tree landed. All had gone as planned except for the fallen branch—but no one could have predicted that. It was an unfortunate hazard of tree-felling…a weak branch could snap and fall from the impact of the axes or the unnatural tilt of the trunk.

People rushed to her, or to the cliff's edge, depending on wherever they were closest to. Those who joined her helped her haul up the rope, while those at the cliff leaned down to offer a hand to Ulrik as he climbed.

The tension eased in her shoulders as he clambered up over the edge, a weary grin on his face as he slapped Bo's shoulder in thanks.

Then he looked towards her and their eyes met. She was the only one still holding on to the rope, and she let it fall from her numb fingers as she called out to her own team, 'Come! We have timber to move!' she shouted, and obediently her people went back to work, the earlier excitement forgotten.

Absently she rubbed her hands down her tunic, only now feeling the burn. Cursing her lack of gloves, she decided to focus her attention back on her own work.

Later that afternoon the sun dropped below the mountain and out of sight, throwing rippling flames across the sky. Most of the timber had been prepared and dragged by ponies back to the workshops. Only a few people remained gathering up tools and preparing to leave.

Ulrik walked by her, and Astrid found herself stopping him. He looked down at where her fingers gripped his wrist.

'Did you hurt yourself when you fell?' she asked quietly, not wanting to draw attention to herself, or show that she cared, but feeling compelled to ask anyway. 'I have some willow bark—if you need it?'

It was the time of her monthlies and she chewed it to ease the painful cramps.

'I am well…a couple of bruises. Nothing more.'

'Your limp seems a little worse,' she argued.

'It usually does after a long day. It is normal…for me.' His head tilted, and she realised he was still staring at her hand wrapped in a strip of linen. The rope had burned both hands, but one of them had begun to bleed, and she'd had to bind it.

'Good.' Dropping his wrist as if he were a hot skillet, she turned away, but he snatched her hand back and lifted it high to examine it better in the fading light.

'You are the one who is hurt, not I,' he said flatly, and it was more of an observation than a question. But a pulse jumped in his throat, suggesting he was more affected by the sight of it than he appeared.

'Light rope burns, nothing serious. My mother has an ointment—it will treat them quickly, and they will be fine by tomorrow… I shall send you some too…for your bruises,' she said, peeling her hand away from the intensity of his blue gaze.

'You did not need to grab the rope. I knew it would hold me.'

She folded her hands across her chest and looked up at the now barren glade. 'I know, it was an accident. Besides, it is nothing compared to what we have done today,' she sighed.

His eyes followed hers to the hillside, covered in the broken wreckage of many felled trees. She had lost count of the number they had cut down today. They had fallen thick and fast once the two important trees had been cut.

'The forest will grow back,' Ulrik said, and she stiffened.

Did he think her a child?

'Of course it will!' she snapped angrily. 'But these oaks were rare and old. I only hope you do them justice with your ship! Otherwise, it would be a terrible waste—'

Ulrik smiled, but it was a sad smile, and she stopped speaking halfway through her rant, realising that she was repeating herself from earlier.

Why could she not speak to him like a normal person?

'Do not worry, Princess. I will make a beautiful ship, worthy of your fine trees. As I am sure you will too.' He stared up into the fading light of the day. 'It is a strange and painful sight...to see the destruction that your own hands have wrought. At least with shipbuilding there is a point...the same cannot be said for other things.'

She shivered at his words. A warrior would understand what he spoke of, but she could only guess. 'It is necessary. Without cutting them down we would have no fuel, or materials to build our homes and ships with. We must do whatever we can to provide for our families,' she said, although why she would try to comfort him with such words was a mystery.

Ulrik nodded and smiled. 'True. But the satisfaction is bittersweet, is it not?'

His words touched her soul and she found herself agreeing with him. 'It is. Whoever planted these is long forgotten, and soon it will be as if they were never here at all...when the pines take over.'

'It is a pity we felled them in spring rather than in the autumn. The dropped acorns might have grown a new grove for you.'

Excitement rose in her chest, lightening her mood. 'My mother always gathers the acorns! Maybe she will have some we can plant?'

'Would that not be a waste of precious time?'

She frowned, her heart falling a little in her chest. *Did she sound silly to him?*

'I suppose it would.'

'Then I will help you. Give me some of your mother's acorns, and I will plant them tomorrow... It is only fair we both give back to the forest.'

Astrid tried to hide her smile but failed, and when she looked at the grizzled man beside her she knocked him playfully with her elbow. 'You are a sentimental old fool!'

He chuckled, and they left the forest together, Astrid feeling content with how well her first day had gone, and not only because she had Revna in her team, or that she had secured the tree that she had wanted all along.

No, it was because of this flickering moment of harmony.

A truce in the twilight that they would probably forget by morning, but that seemed almost a relief to her now.

A rival, but not an enemy.

There was a strange sort of trust balanced between them, and she was glad of it. For all her fire, Astrid longed for peace.

In his opinion, the start of a build was always the most exciting time, because everything was still so uncertain, and yet filled with opportunity. It was probably why he felt so light-hearted this morning.

No, it was more than that...

Working yesterday had made him feel more alive than he had felt in years. Even the background pain of his leg seemed to dim while he laboured, probably because the contest had fired his warrior's heart, and he *wanted* to win.

Not for Frida, or to prove himself against Astrid— although those things were welcome—no, if he were honest with himself, he wanted to win this for himself. To have purpose and pride in his craft. For too long the future had been uncertain, and he'd had to work beneath lesser boat-builders to earn a living.

This was his chance to prove himself.

Already his fingers itched to pick up his blade, to slowly carve away at the trunk in front of his workshop, until he revealed the waiting keel beneath. This ship would be long and wide, he could already see it in his mind's eye.

A ship worthy of a king...or a queen.

His gaze shifted to the hall, and the vibrant figure of Astrid striding down the beach towards him. Had she taken *dagmal* with her parents? It surprised him to see her coming from the hall. She had eaten with her team at the camp last night, and had gone to bed in the smaller longhouse with Revna.

It had not surprised him, as he had heard that before Revna's grandchild had been born the two women had practically lived together in the longhouse he and Frida now occupied.

Rather than begin his day as he had planned, he found himself waiting for her, idly tossing a short-handled axe from hand to hand as he did so. Her direction never faltered, and he realised she was heading straight for him. His heart fluttered, and he smacked the axe head into the trunk, wondering what skirmish she would cause today, and for some reason he looked forward to knowing it.

'I have acorns!' Astrid declared, holding up a sack with one hand and then pushing a clay pot towards him with the other, a carefully constructed look of boredom on her face that almost made him laugh. 'And ointment... My mother swears by it for aches and pains. I thought you might need it after so many falls.'

He took the clay pot from her and put it on a nearby work bench. 'Thank you, but I am perfectly well...it was barely a fall. I merely had to leap and keep hold of the rope. How are your hands?'

It still annoyed him that she had burned her hands trying to save him. Why had she grabbed the rope? He had been so careful, ensuring that the only person in danger would be himself, and yet he'd *still* managed to hurt another, despite his precautions.

'My hands are fine—I slathered them in balm this morning.' She raised them to him and he could see the welts looked a little less red. 'My mother has plenty, so keep the rest for whenever you need it. It will last a couple of months at least. I made it fresh.'

'You made it? I am touched by your concern, Princess.'

Her eyes hardened at the name *Princess*. But he would not use the familiarity she had asked of him— that way led down a worrying path of intimacy. He must always remember who she was, and her status. Every time he used her title it was a reminder to himself of how different they were. Too often he had thought of her in a way that made him uncomfortable, the way a man might appreciate a woman he wished to court.

He had caught himself admiring the occasional strands of chestnut in her dark hair, or the softness of her skin, and it was not only her beauty he had noticed, but also her rich, husky laugh, or how she had leapt to grab the rope, bravely wanting to save him without a moment of hesitation. Her character was as attractive to him as her face was…*worryingly*.

'It was easy enough, and only took a moment. Besides, I needed to go to my mother's stores anyway, for the acorns,' she replied.

'Ahh, yes, the acorns.' He smiled as he thought of their earlier conversation. She was so sweet in some ways, and a she-wolf in others. Her eyes grew wide as she stared up at him, and he wondered if she had ever been kissed. 'You are planting them today?' he asked, pulling his focus away from her and his unwelcome desires.

'I will be going out this morning…you may come if you wish,' she said breezily as she began to walk away, seemingly unconcerned if he would keep his word.

But when he called out to her she stopped, and he knew that she had been waiting to find out. 'Give me a moment, and I will come with you.'

'Are you going into the forest?' asked Frida, stepping out from the doorway, and offering a polite bow to Astrid. 'I would like to gather some mushrooms and moss. May I come with you?'

'Of course, join us!' replied Astrid, turning back to them with a warm smile. He was glad her animosity never seemed directed towards his daughter. In fact, she had been nothing but welcoming to Frida, and he appreciated it.

Ulrik nodded at his daughter to confirm she was allowed. The teams were busy stripping the bark from the logs, and felling other selected pines. There was no need for him to be present, which was probably why Astrid had chosen to do her planting now.

'Thank you, Princess,' said Frida with a bob of her head.

'No need to call me that. My name is Astrid, so call me that—*everyone else* does.' She replied, throwing a glare his way.

Frida gave her a nervous smile, but did not answer. She tended to follow her father's lead in such things. She was an obedient child, and it normally filled his heart with pride, but now he wondered if he should allow her more freedom. His own difficulties with Astrid had nothing to do with her.

The grove looked broken, the twigs beneath Astrid's feet snapping like brittle bones. But it was not as bleak as one might have imagined, and already the insects and birds were busy picking at the fallen leaves and wood shavings, a light hum in the spring air.

Ulrik settled on a spot and dug into the ground with his wooden spade. 'Plant them near the old trunks, but far enough away that the old roots will not stifle them. We do not want these acorns going to waste, especially as they are from the Queen's stores and will not be replenished for many years,' he said to Frida, who nodded nervously.

Not liking the fear in the young girl's eyes, Astrid swung her spade up onto her shoulder, and said cheerfully, 'I will help you, Frida. Then if they fail to flourish it will be my fault not yours, and all my mother will do is throw the last of her acorns at me.'

Frida giggled, and followed her up the hill to begin planting at the top, while Ulrik remained below, planting the lower section.

'Are you sure your mother will not mind so many of her acorns going to waste?' asked Frida quietly. 'Half of these will be dug up by the forest animals.'

'Probably,' smiled Astrid, unconcerned. 'But who could deny Ratatoskr's kin a meal?'

Frida smiled at the mention of the name. 'He is the squirrel that delivers messages up and down the world tree, is he not?'

Astrid stopped at a favourable spot and began to dig. 'Not just messages. Insults and gossip too. Ratatoskr reminds us that once something is said, it can never be unsaid.' Astrid sighed heavily, and not from the exertion of digging. 'Sometimes I wish I remembered that...'

Frida crouched down and placed an acorn in the hole. 'You are strong and opinionated. My father says those are qualities to admire in a woman.'

Astrid covered the hole with soil, then Frida bedded it down firmly with her feet. 'I do not think that your father admires me!' laughed Astrid.

Frida gave a nervous giggle. 'You are the first woman he has really spoken to in many years. He is not very good at it.'

Astrid swallowed a laugh, and focused on finding the next spot to plant. They began to work side by side in a comfortable rhythm, Astrid digging and Frida seeding the ground.

'It is a pity there can only be one shipbuilder,' Frida said quietly. 'I know my father feels bad about challenging your position here.'

If Astrid had been talking with anyone else, she might have said, *Ulrik should feel bad! He should forfeit the challenge and leave!* But this was his young daughter, and she had no right to make her feel guilty for what her father had done.

For once she considered her words before speaking, and realised how true they were. 'If you left, my father would only bring another to replace him. It is not about proving Ulrik's worth, but my own.'

Frida gave her a sympathetic look of understanding that was well beyond her years. 'That is what my father said. Although. he believes this will be his hardest challenge yet…in shipbuilding at least.'

'I am glad he views me as a worthy opponent.' She

glanced down at Ulrik, who was hard at work planting his portion of the acorns.

'What *was* his greatest challenge, then?' Astrid asked curiously, wondering if it was another ship he had built, or even the battle in which he had been badly wounded. She had asked her father about it, and he had said it had been during his campaign against the encroachment of the south-eastern King Sven. Astrid remembered it as one of her father's toughest campaigns, and that many faces had not returned that year.

After a long pause, Frida replied, 'Losing Mother.'

Astrid's shovel paused, and she suddenly felt wretched. Her woes must seem so trivial to Frida. 'I am so sorry. When did she die?'

'Six winters ago. It was an accident.' Frida gave her a brave smile, and looked down towards her father. 'He took it the worst. He still refuses to marry after all this time.'

'I imagine six winters is not that long to grieve for someone. Especially if you loved them deeply.'

'Yes, but Mother would not wish him to be lonely. It is a pity you took Revna for your team. I had hoped they might naturally grow fond of one another. They have similar natures, and have both lost their spouses.'

'Revna?' Astrid barked, shocked beyond words. 'That would never happen.'

She was a grandmother!

'Why not?' asked Frida, who looked a little offended by her words. 'My father may not have a title or wealth, but he is a free man. They would be of equal status, and if my father does win the title of shipbuilder, he will have much to offer her.'

'True, Revna is similar in that she has no family name or wealth to speak of. But even though their status is equal enough, their ages are not. She is too old for your father.'

Frida nodded. 'Perhaps you are right. Maybe one of the thralls, then. He could buy their freedom and make them his wife.'

'They are far too young!' snapped Astrid, not enjoying this conversation one bit. Why did it sour her stomach to think of him courting? It seemed odd that it would anger her like this, although maybe it was purely down to her not wanting him to settle here at all.

'My father is not too old. They had me when they were young.'

'It is impossible for anyone to tell behind all that hair! If he wants a wife, he should go hunting in the forest for a bear—they would make a far better match,' she said, grasping at any reason—no matter how weak—as to why no woman here would be suitable for him.

Frida's shadow flowed over the hole, as if she had stepped closer without realising. But when Astrid looked up, she realised it was Ulrik blocking her light and not Frida.

Astrid was certain that if Odin had transformed her into an acorn in that moment, she would have happily been buried alive.

Ulrik chuckled at Astrid's words and horrified expression. 'I have no need for a wife—bear or otherwise.'

Frida's big eyes stared up at him with concern. 'But Father, who will look after you in your old age?'

Ulrik took more offence at his daughter's words than Astrid's. 'You think me incapable of looking after myself?'

Sensing her father's displeasure, Frida lowered her eyes. 'You will be lonely and…sad,' she said quietly, and he glanced at Astrid, his skin crawling with embarrassment.

'I will be fine.'

Astrid cleared her throat, and swung her spade onto her shoulder. 'You can be lonely and sad even if you are married. My mother is proof of it.'

'They are unhappy?' asked a startled Frida.

Cursing his failure as a father, he gave his daughter a look of warning. 'It is not our place to speak of the King and Queen's marriage.'

'It is well known,' Astrid said with a shrug as she began to lead the way back towards the workshops. 'My mother loved him once. But Viggo is happier at sea, and his absence has hardened her heart to him over the years. Now I think she prefers it when he goes Viking. It is easier for her. When he is gone she can focus on ruling the kingdom, but when he is home she must bend to his will. Even a Queen is subservient to her husband...which I believe is the worst tragedy of all.'

Ulrik and Frida said nothing as they followed Astrid through the well-worn path in silence for some time.

'Mushrooms!' cried Frida, picking up her skirts and clambering up a slope towards a fallen tree covered in the fruit of the forest.

Astrid and Ulrik paused, and waited for Frida to collect what she wanted. 'Marriage is not always like that,' he said, although why he felt compelled to say it was beyond him.

Her eyes slid to his and she gave him a smile, although it did not reach her eyes. 'I would rather not take the chance...besides, I am not suited for such a life. I doubt I would bear it well.'

He had thought himself bitter and cynical, but it

seemed he had met his match. It shocked him that someone so vivacious in all other ways would be so dour about love. 'You are still young…you may feel differently with the right man.'

'I hope not. If my father has his way, they will be a jarl or a king. I doubt they will allow me to roughen my hands with carving.' She raised an eyebrow, silently reminding him that he had said as much himself.

'If he loves you, he will not care as long as you are happy.'

'Did you?' she asked, and a chill ran through him. 'Did you care about what made your wife happy?'

He straightened his spine, accepting the grief and pain willingly. To his surprise it was not as hard to stomach as it usually was. 'I did.'

She nodded with a frown. 'I am not fortunate enough to choose my husband freely, and I doubt the type of man my father picks will care for me.'

'I have never considered myself to be fortunate. Sigrid and I married young after she fell pregnant with Frida. I had very little to offer her, and even less after I was wounded. Although, as we were both from humble families, it did not matter who we fell in love with, or what path we walked in life.'

'I wish I had been so lucky,' grumbled Astrid sourly.

Ulrik's fists clenched and he wanted to shake her until her teeth rattled. Not because she had insulted him, but because she thought so little of herself and her own opportunities. 'No, you do not! I doubt you have ever been hungry, sick, or helpless. Or that you have had to watch the person you love suffer or die because of your own failures—are you so arrogant and spoilt that you are unable to even imagine what it could be like? What am I saying? Of course you do not understand! I will wager you have never wanted for anything. Do not expect any pity from me, *princess!*'

He thought for a moment that she would argue, but instead her face fell and her cheeks flushed a rosy pink. 'I… I am sorry. You are right to reprimand me. I do not know how that would feel.'

Tears were shining in Astrid's eyes and shame clawed at his throat for making her feel bad over something that was not her fault. A movement from the corner of his eye drew his attention to Frida, who stood at the top of the embankment, staring down at him with a horrified expression.

Clearing his throat, he said gruffly, 'I apologise. I know you meant nothing by it, and I spoke too harshly…'

What had possessed him to speak so cruelly?

Revulsion twisted his stomach into knots as he

realised his anger was born out of frustration. He wanted her, could never have her, and so was angry at her for it. His blood turned cold with horror at his own weakness.

Astrid shook her head, and began to walk briskly forward, then over her shoulder she said lightly, 'Thank you for your help with the planting, but I have much to be getting on with, so farewell!'

It did not take her long to move out of sight, and when he looked up at Frida she folded her arms across her chest with a furious expression and said, 'That was unkind of you, Father.'

Ulrik had never hated himself more.

Chapter Nine

Frida approached him carrying a tray. A bowl of water, soap, combs, shears, and a knife gleamed in the morning light, and he sighed with defeat. It appeared he would not make it to noon with his beard intact.

'It is about time you had a trim,' Frida said firmly, her eyes full of steely determination.

'Nonsense!' Ulrik grumbled, even as he sat down on a nearby log and pulled up a stool for her. There was no point arguing with her about it, and yet they always did, probably out of habit. 'Is this because of your conversation with Astrid? I do not wish to marry. So you need not worry about my appearance.'

He glanced towards the other side of the camp, but could not see Astrid. After the planting in the woods yesterday he had only caught glimpses of her. She had been stripping the wood for her keel around the other side of her workshop. He had wondered if it was to avoid him, but dismissed it as ridiculous. Even though his words yesterday had been harsh, he had convinced himself that they could not have cut too deeply. Surely a woman who disliked him so vehemently would not be concerned by his disapproval? Perhaps a little hurt, but she would quickly realise his words held no weight.

Ulrik squirmed in his seat—the reminder of his previous behaviour had stirred up his guilt. He had not slept well the previous night, his mind churning through his words, and remembering the fall of Astrid's face repeatedly.

He should not have been so harsh. He was the one at fault, not her.

Frida shook her head. 'It is not to help you find a wife.'

'Really?' Ulrik asked suspiciously, curious to see what strange reasoning his daughter would come up with.

'Do you not think a master boat-builder should look well-groomed? Should he not reflect the care and beauty of his ships?' She began to attack his hair with the combs and he winced.

'You think King Viggo cares if I trim my hair and beard? Half his warriors are missing teeth!'

'I care!' snapped Frida, yanking the comb through with a vicious tug.

Her anger surprised him. 'But...why?'

'If you refuse to marry, then I will be the woman of this household, and your poor appearance reflects on my skills to manage it. The Queen has sent several bundles of cloth, yet you refuse to let me make anything more for you than one simple tunic! Not to mention the other supplies she has given us. I suspect she believes I cannot manage a household or weave cloth!'

Ulrik was dumbfounded. 'How I dress and groom myself is no reflection on your skills, Frida. You are still a young girl—you haven't even seen fifteen winters yet.'

'I am not far off marriageable age, and you said yourself that you need this position to earn a dowry for me. What man would want me if I cannot even care for my own father?'

Ulrik took her hand in his and tugged her round to face him. 'No man is worthy of you, Frida. But when the time comes—which it will, I am sure—you will have your pick of the best of men, and I will go mad from the constant requests to part with you! Do not wish that day any sooner, I beg you.' She blushed, and swallowed the smile he could tell she was trying hard to hide.

He sighed, and released her hands after a quick squeeze. 'But... I do not wish to embarrass you, and as you say, this is your household. Tidy up your old father if it makes you happy. I am sorry I grumbled about it.'

Frida's eyes softened a little at that, and she began to use the shears on his long beard. 'It is not that I am ashamed of you. It is only that I want to treat you well, and take pride in you as you have always taken pride in me.'

Ulrik closed his eyes and leaned his head back. 'Not too short, otherwise my face itches.'

'Oh, it is all coming off. Maybe then, you will no longer look like an old man!'

He hissed at her teasing, but she ignored him with a chuckle as she began to work.

'Odin's teeth!' Astrid felt as if her heart had dropped into her stomach and then leapt back into place all in the space of one breath.

She may as well have been struck by lightning, the shock of the sight before her was so great. Heat swept up her face and neck, the way it had in the woods after her fall with Ulrik. Shivers of excitement raced over her skin as she stared open-mouthed at the man working at the fire less than fifty feet away.

She rubbed at her eyes to be certain Ulrik hadn't turned into a god visiting from Asgard. 'Is that… *Ulrik*?' she squeaked, horrified by the suddenly high-pitched tone of her voice. Clearing her throat loudly, she tried to make sense of the sight before her.

Revna squinted over at Ulrik, completely untroubled by the sudden appearance of such a handsome man. 'Oh, yes, it looks as if Frida finally got him to shave it off. She did mention she wanted him to look tidier. I think she worries your mother will judge him on his scruffy appearance...you should reassure her about that.'

'She had to make him?' she mumbled, although the question was more to herself. She did not presume to know what it was like to be a man, but surely if she had a face like that she would refuse to hide it from the world. He was...*beautiful!*

Thankfully, he was consumed by his work, otherwise he would have seen her eyes greedily devouring every inch of his face and body. He wore a leather apron, and no tunic. Presumably to avoid its accidentally catching fire as he concentrated on shaping planks for his hull, bending the green wood over the flames with his tools and brute strength. It was a sight that made her feel painfully alive and desperately hollow, all at the same time.

Astrid shook her head, and walked to the piles of timber already split by her crew. She would need to do the same job as Ulrik. There was no avoiding it, and it made sense to use the same fire. But she wondered how she would manage being so close to him.

Just don't look at him, you fool!

After all, he was only a man, it was not as if she had never seen one before…except she couldn't think of anyone that compared to Ulrik.

If she had been a year younger, and a little less wise, then the sight might have overwhelmed her. But the trouble with Bjarni last year had buried any such desires for good. She wasn't built for marriage, and refused to part with her first love—boat-building.

Even before that horrid night, she had been wary. Men tended not to like her boyish manners and twisted sense of humour—some had even mocked her for it. If they did show interest, it was only because they could win great wealth and status by winning her hand—or, at least, that was what her mother always said—and Bjarni's betrayal had confirmed it. He'd tried to win her through force. It had only been a few rough kisses, but it had confirmed her greatest fears.

That wasn't to say she hadn't admired men from afar, or that she was blind to a handsome face. But she was mature enough to put aside her emotions to focus on her work. No man, no matter how handsome, would turn her away from her craft.

So what if he had a fine face and body? She could ignore it!

Yesterday she had revealed her keel, slowly stripping the timber with one of her curve-bladed axes. But now she would need to focus on the hull—the clinker-built shell made with curved planks that would overlap each other, and be secured with rivets and nails.

Of course, the stem and stern logs were always used to calculate the eventual width and depth of the hull. But there was also an art to it, knowing how much a plank would need to be curved by heat before it was laid, and that was always the responsibility of the master builder, so she could not avoid working beside Ulrik.

That morning both teams had put the keel, ribs, stem and stern logs together in a loose working frame, using ropes and clamps to create an outline from which to build around. It was only a rough estimate, but she had marked out the position and bow of the hull, so her team would be busy splitting logs and nailing together the pieces she had prepared.

She couldn't avoid him.

'Better to get on with it, then,' she sighed, picking up her first plank and then making her way over to the fire.

Should she mention his transformation? Would it be strange not to?

He had gone from overgrown bear to handsome man in his prime within the blink of an eye. Acknowledging it seemed obvious, but then, wouldn't that be worse? To show that she had noticed his change in appearance?

She shook her head, trying to clear her wild thoughts, only to see Ulrik look up at her as she approached.

Sapphire eyes pierced her soul and she sucked in a sharp breath.

They were even worse now!

But, no, that was not the end of it, because Ulrik smiled in a friendly welcome, and she felt as if the air had been ripped from her lungs. Two matching dimples formed on his cheeks and she was lost in the beauty of them.

Dimples!

Never would she have imagined something so adorable and enticing to be hidden amongst all that hair.

To her relief, the smile dropped and was replaced with a frown of disapproval. His piercing gaze seemed to witness every wicked thought and feeling that rushed through her body. Could he tell the effect he had on her?

'Why are you not wearing your gloves?' asked Ulrik, as soon as she began to work.

Looking at her bare hands dumbly, she realised she

had forgotten to put her thick leather gloves on as she normally did. Probably too distracted by the sight of Ulrik to realise.

'Oh, yes… I should get them.' She turned to leave but was halted by Ulrik's voice.

'They are in your apron pocket.'

Astrid stared down at the gloves peeking out from the leather, and she silently cursed them for betraying her. 'Ahh, so they are!' She turned back and put them on, taking great care to avoid Ulrik's disconcertingly sharp eyes.

Desiring him was torture! She needed to get back to hating him.

She had to remember that he was an arrogant rival trying to usurp her position, and focus her mind back on the challenge ahead.

Except, each day she found it more of a struggle to hate him. She had gotten to know his sweet daughter, and how much he cared for her. Heard about his lost wife, and the struggles he had faced. Even the way he had reprimanded her yesterday had been reasonable, as she had not suffered as he had, and had no right to claim otherwise.

All he wanted was to build a prosperous life for himself and his daughter. He had proven in only a short time that he was both honourable and brave.

Now, on top of all of that, she could see he was an exceptionally handsome man as well.

It was so unfair!

'Astrid?' His rich voice slid into her thoughts like honey, and her temper flared.

'What?' she snapped, and she swore every worker paused in their hammering before going back to their labours.

Slowly, and with a control that made her heart flutter, Ulrik stopped what he was doing, and stared her down with a heavy dominance that made her feel like a rabbit caught in a trap. It was the kind of powerful look a man might give an insolent youth, or a drunk that had taken a jest too far.

'You are burning it,' he said coldly, and the timber jumped in her hands as she realised what she had done.

The piece was blackened on one end, because she had not been paying attention to it. She dropped it on the ground and stamped out the flames, wishing she could extinguish the last few moments as easily. Ulrik had been trying to help her, and she had kicked at him like a stubborn mule.

She longed to hate him again, to view him as her enemy. Things would be so much easier then.

Looking up at him, she met him with a hard glare of her own. 'It was a rotten piece anyway.'

His jaw clenched and he went back to his own work with a huff of barely contained anger.

Well, then, if she could not hate him, then maybe she would make him hate her instead?

Over the following weeks the hulls of both ships grew and strengthened, until two fat-bellied ships sat next to each other on the shingle beach. Propped up by frames, wedges, and ropes, they were like the skeletons of two whales washed up long ago. Not yet resembling sea-worthy ships, but belonging to the water none the less.

The days stretched longer as spring flowed into summer, and the gentle weather gave them favourable conditions to work in. Astrid's father had left to visit the jarls of his kingdom, and so she felt more at ease. Possibly a little too comfortable, as she had found a pleasant diversion in plaguing Ulrik at every opportunity.

If he had thought her spoilt and childish before, her recent behaviour would have only confirmed it, and she did not care.

Better for him to hate her and, more importantly, for her to hate him.

The first few days of their meeting had worried her. They were rivals, and she wanted them to remain that way. Her tricks and petty acts of war had amused and reassured her of the impossibility of their ever being amicable with one another.

One day, Ulrik's axe would go missing and be found wedged in the side of the privy, or he might find his tool bag hidden beneath a pile of logs, or his tunic and apron pegged out in the incoming tide.

It was never anything harmful, or that would be detrimental to the build of his ship. No tools or materials were ever damaged in any way. Just minor, petty inconveniences and games. Her goal was to torment, not break her opponent. To remind them both that they were enemies.

The only other rule she stuck by was that Frida should not suffer for her tricks. She still felt bad about the timber in their home, and did not want to burden the young girl any more than she had. After their fall in the forest, she had asked Inga to send them extra supplies to make up for it, as well as plenty of cloth to replace the tunic she had ripped in their fall, and possibly give Frida a couple of extra dresses as a silent apology for the timber. Although she hoped neither of them suspected it was her doing, and had made her mother promise not to reveal it either. It would ruin the bad reputation she had so carefully built for herself.

To her surprise and disappointment, Ulrik never

retaliated against her, not once, and so her games had grown more ridiculous in recent days.

At the start of the week, after much searching, his bucket of nails had been found on the roof of his house. Two days later, he had woken to find his wedges laid out in a circle around his home, and yesterday he had found a cock and balls drawn in charcoal on his stern.

So common were her tricks that she no longer hid her part in them, and even moved things in front of his crew without fear of reprisal. After all, they had known her all her life, knew there was no real malice in her actions. They merely shook their heads with an indulgent smile at her odd behaviour.

Ulrik, too, seemed undisturbed by her nonsense, and would simply ask loudly where his latest missing item was, and wait for a response like, *Have you tried the chicken coop, Master Ulrik?*

Everyone was always happy to help him, especially the female thralls of the camp, who had shown a sudden interest in Ulrik ever since his beard had been shaved. Astrid would have laughed at their shallowness if she weren't so embarrassed by her own visceral reaction to him—it was bad enough that she had found her enemy intriguing before, but now her attraction almost felt obscene in its ridiculousness.

So her tricks grew in number, and Ulrik's reaction remained steadfast, merely giving a light nod of thanks to those who helped him, and then trudging off without complaint.

Of course, if he had sent word to her father or even threatened to tell him, it would have immediately stopped. But he seemed content to let her have her way, and a part of her was even a little disappointed. Not because she welcomed her father's eventual punishment—he would probably force her to down tools for the day, or something similar. No, mainly it was because if he did retaliate, then at least she would have one good reason to hate him.

Chapter Ten

Ulrik stared down at the rib he had been working on. Rather than the small axe he had left in the piece mid-cut, one of his hair combs now sat wedged in its place. He plucked it out of the groove and examined it to see if it had been damaged.

'You will be sawing all day and night if you think that's the right tool for the job,' Astrid said mildly as she passed by with her own axe lightly resting on her shoulder. 'You might want to try using an axe instead?'

He refused to give her the satisfaction of letting her see his frustration. A fire could not burn without fuel. Instead, he did as he always did: he silently listed the names of Loki's children to himself.

Hel, Jörmungand, Fenrir, Sleipnir and... Astrid.

Of course, the last one wasn't for certain, but as each day passed, he was more convinced that the trickster god *was* her real father.

He had thought by ignoring her that she would eventually grow bored. But he feared his own patience would snap well before she tired of her teasing.

'Master Ulrik, I will help you find it—I think I saw it in the cold store,' said Brenna, one of the thrall women who helped manage the camp.

Astrid threw a disgruntled look her way, but Brenna seemed untroubled by the Princess's reaction, and Ulrik gave her a grateful smile. 'Thank you... I seem to be quite forgetful these past few weeks.'

Brenna returned his smile with a rosy blush. 'I am always happy to help you, Master...*with anything.*'

Astrid gave a loud snort of disgust as she walked away, and Ulrik cleared his throat awkwardly. This wasn't the first time Brenna had flirted with him, and, like the teasing from Astrid, he had tried to ignore it in the hope that it would eventually disappear.

'I am sure I can find it. In the cold store, did you say?'

But Brenna seemed determined to come with him, as she hurried after him. 'Let me show you—the store is so full with supplies, it might take you until Ragnarök to find it.'

He glanced at her, surprised that she would mention the Norse term for the end of the world. 'I thought you were Anglo-Saxon.'

'Oh, I am originally, but I have lived here most of

my life, since I was captured as a child, and I have accepted Odin into my heart,' she said with a sincerity that surprised him. 'And,' she continued, 'if I was ever lucky enough to be freed, I would gladly teach my children the sagas.'

Ulrik gave a pleasant nod, whilst praying that his axe would be easy to find. The cold store was a chamber dug deep into the ground and walled with rocks. So he grabbed a torch from the fire before making his way towards it. Brenna seemed content to follow him.

'I do not think my freedom would cost much. The Queen has always liked me…' continued Brenna, and Ulrik suddenly felt very sorry for her.

'I am sure she does.'

The torch cast very little light in the store, and they moved around it slowly, checking the storage pots and baskets.

Brenna gave a delighted gasp as she pulled the axe from the butter churn she'd been looking in. 'Here it is!'

He reached for it, and her hand held on to it tightly. 'Would you consider me, Master? As a wife? I know we are not long acquainted, but I would ask that you at least think on it. I am good at weaving cloth, and running a home.'

Ulrik stared at Brenna in shock. 'I may not win

the challenge...' he said, unsure of how to reject her without offending her.

'I am sure you will,' she said, her voice confident. 'The King does not want her to win.'

'I... I am honoured...but...'

Immediately Brenna's face brightened, although he could see the sadness beneath her smile. 'No need to answer me yet. I only ask that you consider me. Nothing more.' She handed him the axe and he hooked it onto his belt, glad for something to do.

In truth, he could not think of any reason to reject her. Brenna was everything he should want in a woman. She was pretty with her flaxen hair and hazel eyes, hardworking, and only slightly younger than himself.

For years he had never imagined remarrying, partly because he did not wish to replace Sigrid, and partly because no woman would have had him as a poor labourer. But if he did become master boat-builder... maybe he should.

The idea did not seem as strange as it once had, and did he truly wish to live a life alone once Frida left home?

But for some reason he still flinched at the idea of marrying Brenna, even though everything about her was appealing, and reminded him a little of Sigrid. Idly he tried to imagine making love to her, but it was Astrid's features that came to mind. He shook his head, wondering if all the tricks were beginning to scramble his thoughts.

Astrid was beautiful, young, wild, and completely unattainable. She was a princess and so far from his own status that she may as well be the daughter of a god. Not only that, but it was also clear she despised him.

The image of her lying beneath him in the forest rose unwelcome in his mind.

She had liked him then, if only a little.

His body stiffened as he remembered the gleam of lust in her eyes that day. Innocent, and yet hungry for a pleasure she didn't fully understand. He sighed, trying his best to push the unwelcome thoughts from his mind.

He had no right to think of her in such a way. Besides, his future, and Frida's future, depended on his beating her.

Brenna misunderstood the grim look on his face as they emerged from the cold store. 'Why do you let her do it?' she whispered. 'I know she is the Princess, but if you sent word to her father...or even spoke to the Queen—'

'No.' He shook his head firmly.

'But—'

When Ulrik answered, he was surprised by his own

words, he had not realised the full reason behind his lack of action until now. 'Let her have her tricks—she has no other way of punishing me, and she will tire of them eventually. Speaking to her parents would be taking an unfair advantage over her.'

'She has no good reason to punish you—she agreed to the contest.'

'Because she had no choice. I am glad to have this opportunity, but the truth is...she deserves her place here, and it should never have been put into question.'

Brenna frowned, but then gave a light shrug of agreement. 'I suppose...but you are wrong if you think she will tire of plaguing you. Princess Astrid is relentless!'

Brenna's expression grew more confused when he said with a smile, 'You are right...maybe I should give more thought to how to end these games?'

As he made his way back to the camp fire he caught Astrid's narrowed eyes watching him darkly. With a cheerful smile he held his axe high in the air. 'I found it!'

Astrid felt as if she had swallowed glass. None of her tricks had worked to rattle Ulrik, and she couldn't believe how obvious Brenna's flirtations had been. Then again, Brenna probably had to act quickly—the other thralls were swarming around him like flies around fresh meat as it was.

Not that he seemed to notice, or that she should care.

Why did she care?

She liked Brenna, and her mother also thought highly of her. Normally she would have encouraged Brenna to court a man like Ulrik. The woman had been desperate for a husband for many years. Sadly, her father's warriors had always given Brenna false promises in exchange for bed favours. She doubted Ulrik would do such a thing—he was an honourable man after all.

The afternoon flowed slowly into dusk, and she still felt no better about seeing Ulrik and Brenna emerge from the cold store together. As it was another dry night, the teams gathered around the outside fire, sitting on logs to eat their meal, and watch the sun sink into the rippling water together. The supplies were usually sent down by her mother in the late afternoon, and Frida had taken to managing them, creating hearty stews that were always delicious and filling.

A hefty catch of salmon and trout had been dropped at Frida's door earlier, and the fragrant fish stew had drawn all the workers away from their tools early. The arrival of a cask of her father's ale added to the cheerful mood, and she wondered if her mother had heard about her tricks and wished to ease some of the tension.

Everyone dug into their meals, and Astrid's heart raced as Ulrik came to sit beside her. She turned her body away from him, knowing that he probably only sat beside her because Frida was on the same log.

She preferred not to look at him too closely these days. He was still clean shaven, his dark hair neatly chopped at his shoulders and tied back. Each morning, after eating *dagmal*, he sat for Frida as she shaved his beard and combed his hair. It was an oddly sweet moment between father and daughter that always fascinated Astrid. She doubted her own father would sit so serenely for her while she held a blade at his throat.

'May I ask you something, Princess?'

Astrid stopped mid-bite and raised her eyes. Ulrik and Frida were looking at her with equal intensity, as if she were a Norn about to proclaim their fates.

'Speak freely,' she mumbled, returning to her meal, and trying her best to ignore the heat of his body beside her.

'The food supplies…' He paused, and she noticed the little nervous inhale Frida made beside him. 'Frida and I were wondering if they were due to your presence here. If the Queen was simply ensuring her youngest daughter was being well cared for?'

Astrid nodded. 'I expect so. Why?'

Frida visibly sagged with relief, although her hands were still twisted in her apron. 'Only...the Queen has sent her personal servants to help with the cooking and cleaning...'

Oh, the thralls are more than happy to help! Astrid thought bitterly, remembering Brenna's eagerness earlier to help Ulrik. But she tempered her reply, not wanting to upset Frida. 'There are over twenty mouths to feed down here. My mother would not expect you to manage alone, and everyone here is busy with the shipbuilding.'

'Yes, but today we have received a lot! There is so much fish I will need to smoke the leftovers, and the women are the Queen's special servants! Also... the ale...' There was worry in Frida's eyes, and Astrid finally understood what the poor girl was concerned about.

'My mother probably hoped I would return to the hall each night. I told her recently that I would not, as I wish to be close to my work...' lied Astrid. 'She is probably helping with provisions and labour to ease my burden from your shoulders. Please do not see this as any reflection on your ability to run a household. For anyone, this would be considered too large a duty.' She waved meaningfully at the camp.

Frida shook her head fiercely. 'Honestly, I am

happy to do it. There is no need for the Queen's ladies to help as well—I am sure I can manage.'

Ulrik took Frida's hand and gave it a light squeeze. 'Accept the Queen's help, sweetheart. It would be rude to turn it away.'

Astrid's heart ached for the girl. She was still so young, and yet she was worried others thought her incapable of running her own home, which was ridiculous. Astrid was an adult and she wouldn't even know where to start preparing a meal for so many. She had never bothered to learn.

'In truth,' Astrid said thoughtfully, drawing Frida's attention, 'my mother must think very highly of you not to have immediately offered her assistance. She must have seen how well you had managed sorting out your home that first day, and trusted you to manage alone with only the supplies she gave you. But now that I have insisted on eating and sleeping here every night she probably feels compelled to offer more.'

Frida's eyes brightened with hope. 'Do you really think so?'

Astrid gave her a reassuring smile. 'I am certain of it.'

She grinned as she stood up. 'I made some stewed berries. Let me get them.'

'Frida,' Astrid called out before the girl walked away. 'Remember, you are not alone here. We are a community, we help each other. There is never any shame in asking for guidance.'

After Frida had gone, Ulrik said quietly, 'Thank you, Princess.'

'I meant every word,' Astrid said firmly, mopping up the last of her meal with a chunk of bread.

'I know, but she needs to hear it from someone other than me. Sometimes, she can take too much upon herself. It was…kind of you.'

Astrid blinked and almost choked on her bread. No one had ever called her kind before. She shrugged off the compliment. 'She is a sweet girl. You raised her well.'

Ulrik's jaw tightened, and he gave a gruff nod. 'Thank you, but I am not sure I deserve such praise.' At her disbelieving look, he added, 'You see, there was a long time after my wife died…when I didn't look after Frida as I should have. She took it upon herself to look after me, when I should have been caring for her. She still bears the weight of that responsibility.'

Astrid stared down into her bowl, wishing he would not tell her such things. It only made her heart ache for him. 'That is understandable—you were both grieving, and maybe it was the only way she could manage her own pain. When I am sad, I like to stay busy…' She moved quickly on before she revealed too much.

'I suspect she is the same. Do not let the past burden you. Frida does not. I think she takes great pride in you, and your achievements.' Instinctively Astrid reached out and patted his thigh in a friendly gesture. A look of horror crossed his face, and she quickly snatched her hand away.

'There is no need to act so disgusted! I only meant it kindly!' she grumbled, secretly pleased to finally have some reason to bite back at him.

'I...' Ulrik stared at her, his eyes wide. 'I could never be disgusted by you... I was surprised, that is all.'

Wishing to change the direction of this odd conversation, Astrid asked bluntly, 'Do you have a spare moulding iron?'

'Is this why you were being kind to Frida?' He sighed. 'Because you want something from me?'

Astrid rolled her eyes at his outrage.

Why must he always think the worst of her?

Except, wasn't that what she wanted? Somehow it was not as satisfying as she had imagined it to be. 'Of course not, she is a lovely girl. I have no cause to say a single word against her... Do you have a spare moulding iron, or not?'

'I have two.'

'You do?' Astrid grinned. 'Can I buy it from you? Mine broke earlier today.'

'It is not for sale.'

Anger sparked inside of her and she thumped her bowl down on the ground. 'But you have two! Why would you need both?'

'I don't.' Ulrik smiled slyly. She slapped his bicep, hating the slight sting his rock-hard muscle gave her palm. Not to mention the tingle of awareness that also ran through her as she remembered the sight of his bare arms.

'Then let me have it! Or at least…tell me what I must do to get it. A new one will take days to make!'

He leaned forward, until there was only a breath between them. 'I want an end to the *little elves.*'

She frowned, wondering if they were even talking about the same thing any more. 'Little elves?'

'Yes, the elves that keep moving my tools, and playing tricks on me!'

Astrid thought carefully before speaking. 'Well, I do not know of any *elves*, but I am sure I can make an offering in the forest—which should appease them.'

'Hmm,' he replied, obviously unsatisfied by her answer, his head tilted in a very distracting way as he stared straight into her eyes as if searching for deceit.

'I am sure it will work!' she cried, a little desperate now.

'I do not think an offering will be enough,' he said with a heavy sigh that was rich and husky.

'And what will be enough?' she asked, biting her lip, and wondering why her chest suddenly felt so tight.

As if distracted, he dropped his eyes and they lingered on her mouth. The silence between them stretched, and she swore she could hear her heart thundering in her chest as she waited for him to speak.

Firelight flickered across the hard line of his mouth, and she found herself examining him like one of her sculptures. Her eyes trailed away from the bow of his lips, up to the square angle of his jaw, then down to the smooth plain of his neck and the knot of his throat. If only he would smile again, she would see his dimples and he would be...

Perfect.

He swallowed, and she blinked, realising too late that he was not a sculpture, but a living, breathing man. One that would not wish to be lusted after, especially by his rival.

'You can have it,' he said, his voice so deep and rough she wondered if she had misheard him.

'What?'

'The moulding iron—have it. But swear to me that will be an end to your *games.*' The last word was spat out with a bitterness that made her body stiffen. Maybe she had rattled him after all?

She gave a dumb nod, unsure of what else to say.

She had the uneasy feeling her tricks were not the only thing to trouble him.

The problem was, if she were playing a game, she had no idea how to win.

Chapter Eleven

'Where is my moulding iron?' bellowed Ulrik, his irritation threatening to boil into rage.

Frida gave him a blank look, as did a couple of the nearby thralls, who shrugged their shoulders, and half-heartedly began looking through the work-bench tools.

'If she has gone back on her word...' Ulrik hissed a savage curse under his breath that made Frida jump and hurry to help in the search. He stopped her with a gentle touch on her arm. 'I will find it.'

He hated that he had made her nervous.

'I will look in the longhouse,' Frida said with a quick nod of determination before heading inside.

Ulrik's fists clenched at his sides.

No more games!

Astrid had agreed, and yet here he was—only a few days later—missing the one tool he needed!

The tricks Astrid had previously played on him

had been a mild irritation that had not bothered him greatly as no real harm had come from them. Sometimes he even found them amusing, especially the more ridiculous jests. But this time it would interfere with his work, and not only that—for her to break her word so quickly…?

Well, it was childish and spiteful even for that vixen! And he was *done* with indulging her! Someone who gave false promises was the worst kind of person in his mind, and he was angry and disappointed that Astrid would prove to be so rotten.

What an idiot he had been! Indulging in her whims for this long, and why? Because he felt sorry for the spoilt Princess… Well, that would end now!

The workshops were quiet today. More trees needed felling, as they had run out of the pine planks and needed more. There was an abundance of pine here, so he had left the felling of the trees to Bo and the rest of his team, while he began work on carving his figurehead. Astrid had done the same, as her team had also left early, and he could see that her tools were all laid out beside her, including the spare moulding iron he had given her…*stupidly,* for now he had nothing to use.

'Princess!' he shouted, the word booming out across the camp and causing Astrid's shoulders to jump. He refused to pity her a moment longer—his patience was dead and buried.

His anger kicked like a mule in his chest and propelled his feet forward. Storming over to her, he was determined not to waste a moment longer on her pettiness and lies.

Astrid squinted up at him as he approached, having to shield her eyes from the mid-morning light. 'What is wrong with you?'

'My moulding iron is missing. Where is it?' He held out his hand expectantly.

'How should I know?' she snapped back, and he noticed the possessive way she picked up the spare one he had given her. Lightly she began scratching into the surface of her timber, but he could tell she had only wanted to hold it out of his reach. 'Maybe it is in the pack Bo took with him? He did seem as if he were throwing everything in there.'

'Did you put it in there?' he growled, and she had the nerve to look offended.

'I did not! I do not even know if he took it—have you checked in your longhouse?'

'Get it now!' he said coldly, his jaw painfully tight. His temper was on a fragile leash, and her continued deceit did nothing to cool it. 'Or I will take back my spare!' he warned.

Her eyes widened with horror. 'You cannot! I am using it!'

'If you refuse to tell me where you have hidden mine, then I will have it back!'

'I did not take it!' she cried, jumping to her feet, and glaring up at him.

'I will not waste a full day's carving because of you! You swore you would not play any more tricks!'

Her face was flushed, but he did not know if it was from anger or guilt. 'I am telling you the truth. I have not touched it!'

'Give me that!' he barked, reaching for the moulding iron.

'No! You said I could have it!' She jumped away, holding the tool tightly and a little behind her as if she were protecting a child.

'You did not keep your part of the bargain, and I want it back!' He walked towards her and she backed further away, walking through her workshop and into the longhouse, as if the sanctity of her home could protect her.

When she moved to slam the door in his face, he stopped it with the slap of his palm and pushed it forward, following her inside.

He had never been in her longhouse. Unsurprisingly it was sumptuously furnished. Beautiful tapestries, furs and blankets covered the walls, chairs, and beds. All gifts from the Queen, and the sight of such luxury only angered him further. She could pay for a thousand moulding irons, so why must she keep his?

'I will have it back, even if I have to hold you down to take it!'

Gasping in outrage, she said, 'You only want it back because you lost your own! I am not to blame for that. I did not touch it and I have no idea where it is.'

Her words seemed sincere, but her past behaviour tarnished them in his eyes. Moving closer, he began to press forward, hoping to intimidate her enough so that she gave up and handed it back.

Why was she fighting him on this?

Her bottom knocked into the table behind her, and a water jug rocked from side to side, threatening to fall. He stilled it by reaching around her to place his palm firmly on top. Astrid gave a startled squeak and danced away to the side.

'Enough of this nonsense! Give it back now…you are wasting time, although I am sure you are aware of that already, as you seem determined to waste mine!'

She backed further away, holding the moulding iron as far away from him as possible. Sick of her games, he strode forward and made a grab for it.

Thumping his chest, she tried to push him away with her free hand, which proved useless, and he grabbed her wrist and tugged her close.

'Damn you!' she spat. 'It is mine!'

They grappled together, each trying to snatch it from the other's grasp. In the struggle, Astrid's foot knocked against his shin, and although it did not hurt, he shifted his weight and ended up unbalanced. When she arched away from him, he tried to wrap his arm around her to stop her falling, but their fate was already set and, like before, they fell together.

At least this time it was a soft landing.

Her bed was piled high with rare northern furs, silk embroidered blankets from the east, and downy pillows that threw white fluff into the air as they collapsed on top of one another, the wooden bed creaking loudly under the strain.

Feathers fluttered around them like snowflakes, the only sound between them their laboured breath as they stared into each other's eyes. Pressed against one another, Ulrik lay on top of her, the precious moulding iron still gripped in both of their hands high above their heads.

He sucked in a breath, trying to focus his mind, but his heart was still thundering in his chest, and she felt far too pleasant beneath him. Soft, lush, and rare, she was like the fabrics draped all over the bed. Arousal hit him in a wave of longing and he realised how empty his own bed had been for so many years.

Astrid's lips called to him. He had imagined kissing her more than once. The soft curves were always pouting or mocking him with sly smiles, and the temptation to taste them was overwhelming.

Her breath was coming out in short pants, its warmth fluttering against his neck in a carnal way that had an immediate effect on his body, and he winced. Shifting his weight onto his forearms, he repositioned himself, to help her breathe more easily.

Perversely, he kept his lower body lightly pressed against hers, conscious that he must be heavy on top of her, but unwilling to lose his grip on his prize.

Although what was the prize?

Was it the moulding iron, or Astrid pinned beneath him? He was no longer sure of anything, and that worried him. He slid his fingers down to encircle hers.

Warning beacons flared in his mind.

He had no right to touch her, no right to take anything from her, especially not a kiss!

But they may as well have been seen through a thick blanket of fog for all the attention he paid them, because when he saw his own passion reflected in her eyes, his body stiffened and he could no longer deny either of them.

Dipping his head until there was only the smallest whisper of air between them, he pressed his mouth against hers and waited. He was giving her a choice.

In the silence of that unanswered question their bodies shared breath and heat.

Although his lower body was pressed against hers, in no other way was she restrained. She was free to slap the outrageous presumption from his mind, as well as the opportunity and permission to reject him. He was certain that would be easier to bear than this uncertainty.

Then, unbelievably, she arched towards him, and their lips brushed for a second time, in a gentle and tender caress. Her eyes widened, and then closed. Dreamily, as if it was not only an acceptance, but also a relief. The moulding iron was forgotten as she slipped her arms around his neck and pulled him closer, curving her body against his.

All doubt and uncertainty were swept away in a rush of bittersweet longing. He needed to feel the press of her body against his, desperately wanted to explore her mouth with his tongue. To his shock she answered his every desire, parting her lips and pressing against him with an urgency that took his breath away.

But he was no longer a green youth without control, and he gentled her with a tender stroke down her face and neck, encouraging her to savour and explore the passion between them. For he knew that patience gave its own rewards.

Slowly, he deepened the kiss, all previous temper forgotten. But Astrid was impatient and her hips tilted up to his insistently. He pushed her back down, calming her whimper with a tender kiss in the hollow of her neck, rocking against her until he wrung a moan from her lips.

Frida's call from outside dashed his lust like a bucket of icy water. 'Father! I think Bo is returning from the forest... I think he has your moulding iron!'

Raising himself up onto his elbows, Ulrik gasped in horror and looked towards the doorway. Thankfully, it was closed and Frida had not come in to tell them of Bo's return, but his stomach twisted painfully when he thought about what his daughter would think of such a sight.

Odin's teeth! What was he thinking?

Glancing down at himself, and then up at the timber ceiling, he groaned at the visible proof of his lust, and stumbled to his feet.

Astrid's eyes grew wide with concern as she gasped, 'Are you hurt?'

'No,' he mumbled, turning away from her, 'but I should be.'

When had he ever let his passions rule him like this? He had been celibate since the death of Sigrid and the lack of intimacy had not bothered him. Now he feared that his desire for Astrid ran far deeper than he could have ever thought possible.

Of all the women to stir his soul back to life after so many years, why did it have to be her?

Astrid, a princess, and his rival. The gods were laughing at him, he was certain of it.

'Forgive me, Princess, that should not have happened, and I swear it will *never* happen again.'

Why did his voice sound so cold?

Astrid was still struggling to think straight after that toe-curling kiss, but he had already stood, and was apparently done with whatever had just passed between them.

Astrid was not so lucky. She lay dazed on her bed, wondering why it suddenly felt so empty and alone.

No, not her bed, *she* felt empty and alone. The realisation sent a whip of pain down her spine and she sat up stiffly. Tartly she replied, 'I told you. I never touched your moulding iron!'

His shoulders slumped. 'I am sorry.'

She laughed, desperately hoping she sounded carefree. No matter what, she would never let him know his rejection had hurt her. 'Well, the kiss was nice... if brief. You really are a strange man, Ulrik. You change direction as quickly as the wind! There is no need to apologise—it meant nothing to me. You are not the first man to let his passion get the better of him in my presence.'

'What do you mean?' he asked, turning to frown at her, and she laughed.

Tossing the moulding iron from hand to hand, she shrugged. 'Only that you are not alone in wanting to strangle me one moment, and bed me the next.'

He looked genuinely appalled. 'I would never hurt you.'

Too late.

Every day he hurt her, when he called her *Princess* in that snide tone of his. As if he could not bear to think of her as a normal person with thoughts and feelings. He looked repulsed by his attraction to her and that stung.

Spoilt and childish, that was what he thought of her, and she hated it, and she hated *him!*

As she passed him, she tossed her braid over her shoulder and gave him a wide, teasing smile. 'You are a surprisingly good kisser, you know. I almost forgot how annoying you are.' She paused thoughtfully. 'I wonder what my father would say, if I told him...'

Ulrik paled, and her stomach tightened, because this time she was the one disgusted—with herself. Patting him on the shoulder, she said reassuringly, 'Do not worry. As I said, it meant *nothing*. Enjoy the rest of your day, Ulrik. I certainly will...'

Let him choke on that!

She left the room carrying so much false confidence that she sagged against the side wall straight after, burdened by its weight. Hidden out of sight, she sank to a crouch and sucked in three heavy breaths. Her knuckles were bone-white as she gripped the moulding iron, her victory as hollow as her pride.

'Do not let him rattle you!' she muttered to herself, but her fingers trembled.

'Astrid?'

She leapt a foot in the air when she heard her name, but as soon as she realised it was Revna she grabbed the woman's hand and ran.

Revna, who was used to Astrid's impulsive nature, merely smiled indulgently, and followed obediently until they stopped behind the longhouse. 'Why are you hiding from him?' she asked eventually, when Astrid had peeked around the corner more than once already.

Astrid sucked in a deep breath as if she were preparing herself for battle, and not about to confess her secret shame. 'Ulrik... I kissed him, or did he kiss me? I am not even sure... No, he kissed me first, I am certain of it.'

Revna chuckled. 'Then why are you here?'

Astrid scowled. 'What?'

'Was it bad?' Revna raised an eyebrow, and Astrid choked on her indignation.

'What does it matter? We both regretted it.'

Revna nodded thoughtfully, and kicked absently at the ground. 'How long shall we wait?'

Sighing, Astrid sank against the back wall and stared up at the sky. There was plenty of daylight left, and still much work to be done. She could not hide from him forever. 'Until I learn to hate him again.'

Revna sat on the log pile beside her, rearranging her skirts to be more comfortable. 'Do you remember when you first came down here? You must have only seen ten or eleven winters. Your mother was so busy with young Viggo, and your sisters were infatuated with the jarls your father had brought home.'

'I remember.' *She had been so lonely.*

'And then you helped Garold with his carvings, and stayed longer every day. I was terrified your mother would be angry with us.'

'She was glad you were looking after me. No one else had time. My sisters were obsessed with finding husbands, and my mother knew her time with Young Viggo was coming to an end. She indulged his difficult ways a little too often, knowing that she would miss him terribly when Father began his training...'

Astrid laughed. 'She indulged me too, in her way. I was a difficult sister, impatient with my brother, always running wild. Maddening poor Bodil and Liv with my teasing.' The tricks she had played on Ulrik were nothing compared to those days.

'You wanted their attention.'

Astrid felt her stomach flip, and she dropped down on the logs beside Revna feeling as if her legs had been kicked out from beneath her. After a pause, she whispered, 'I am pathetic.'

Revna wrapped an arm around her shoulders and pulled her close. 'Obsession is a strange beast. Our ships could never have been built so well, or sailed so far without it. Never be ashamed of your passionate nature, but do try to understand it. Your constant teasing of Ulrik is because you want him to notice you.'

'I hate him, I do not *want* him!' Astrid snorted. 'He is my rival, and I…' She struggled to find the words.

'You are fascinated by him.'

'I *need* to prove that I am better than him.'

'Why?' Revna asked with a knowing eye. 'Because your father thinks him better?'

Astrid nodded, and then added, 'And so does Ulrik.'

'Hmm, I do not think so. I think he thinks very highly of you…too highly probably.'

Astrid snorted again, and kicked at the dusty ground.

'Come!' Revna stood and slapped her hands together. 'Shall we go back to our work? Maybe, if you keep your hands busy, your heart will decide the best path to take.'

Astrid rose with a glum nod and followed her, her stomach still twisting with the words Revna had forced her to accept. 'Yes, but I already know what I must do. I should focus on my ship—that is where my heart belongs. Ulrik is just a distraction.'

Chapter Twelve

Ulrik stared at the two half-finished ships propped up on the beach in front of him. The last few weeks had passed quickly, with no further clashes between him and Astrid. They seemed content to ignore and avoid each other.

Which was impossible in such a small camp, but they had somehow managed it, both focusing on their builds, and pretending the other did not exist, even though he felt her presence keenly, and had to stop himself from searching for her whenever he turned away from his labour.

At least both dragon ships were taking shape, with shallow bellies, tall necks and tails. The hoists and timber scaffolding surrounding each ship were impressive in themselves, rising high into the air, and dwarfing the men who climbed them.

Each ship had nine strakes so far, the constant hammering of the nails filling the air with a continuous rhythm. Each rivet needed a hundred strikes of the hammer, and there would be hundreds of nails in each hull by the time it was complete. The clinking of the hammers gave the hull its name, clinker-built.

The smell of tar and singed hemp filled the air, from all the joints that had been welded together, but Ulrik found he rather liked the acrid stench. It reminded him of his purpose and eventual goal, something he had recently begun to struggle with.

His ship would be wider than Astrid's, as his oak keel had suited a more substantial hull. Astrid's seemed to be narrower and sleeker in comparison. Quicker in the water perhaps, but it might not carry as heavy a load, although that was a question far too early to contemplate.

Strangely, he did not spend much time comparing the ships, and instead seemed obsessed with recalling over and over the taste of Astrid's kiss and the press of her body against his. He savoured the memory, even as it twisted and unravelled his thoughts each night. While his boat was taking shape, his mind, in contrast, seemed to be falling apart.

As the days stretched from spring into summer, he learned the startling differences between his old home and new. The midsummer sun would not set this far north. According to Bo, it merely dimmed to a magical twilight for only a few hours each night. Ulrik was used to long summer days in Aalborg, but here the days were never-ending, and both teams worked until late. He wondered how he would sleep, but Bo had laughed and said the time for rest would come in the winter, when there would be no daylight at all.

Ulrik now understood the northerners' love for the upcoming summer festival much better. The building crews talked about it endlessly, and Frida seemed to be looking forward to it with as much anticipation and excitement as the rest of the settlement, who were all eagerly preparing decorations and gathering in food from all over the kingdom.

A great bonfire was being built on one of the hill-sides overlooking the harbour, and as soon as the King returned it was going to be lit, banishing any evil spirits that planned to do the kingdom harm during the autumn and winter months, as well as being a celebration and a thank-you to Frey and Freya for their divine blessing over the harvest.

Tonight everyone was eating boiled chicken with leeks and prunes, gobbling it up with the oatcakes sent down from the hall as they chatted by the fire.

To everyone's astonishment, Bo made a surprising announcement. 'I am going to tell Skadi how I feel,' he said, with a deep and profound sigh of resignation. As if he were swearing to kill a man, and not to proclaim his love for a woman.

Shocked gasps filled the air, and Ulrik noticed Astrid's was one of them. She sat on the same log as him, less than an arm's length away. She had come to the campfire late like himself, and so had no choice but to sit with him, otherwise he was sure she would not have.

'You are?' she prodded, leaning forward and staring at Bo in amazement.

Ulrik had gotten to know Bo over their time building together, and had thought the blacksmith likeable, if quiet.

Bo nodded, although the poor man looked sickened by the prospect. 'We have danced around each other for long enough. I know how I feel and I do not think I can stand another winter in the hall wondering if she feels the same. Besides, the midsummer festival brings good luck to lovers...'

'It does!' said Brenna from across the fire, and Ulrik quickly looked away when he saw her shy smile directed towards him.

Astrid grinned warmly at Bo, as if she had not seen or heard Brenna. 'I will wish you luck, Bo. She would be an idiot not to accept you. Honestly, I am surprised you have not asked her before now. You have been in love with her for years!'

Bo gave a shy smile, his large shoulders relaxing a little at Astrid's confidence in him. 'I will still guard you during the festivities though, Princess. I mean to speak with Skadi before the lighting of the bonfire.'

Astrid nodded, a mischievous look in her eye that was in complete contrast with the seriousness of her words. 'I have already sharpened my blades.'

'Why would you need to sharpen your blades?' asked Ulrik curiously. Normally he would have ignored any conversation involving Astrid, as she did with him, but the mention of sharpening blades gave him an uneasy feeling.

Astrid shrugged, avoiding his gaze as she stirred her bowl with her spoon. 'One of the jarls might get over-confident during the festival. It is nothing serious.'

Revna leaned forward, her eyes searching his face as she said in a hard voice, 'Last time, one of the jarl's sons, Bjarni, locked Astrid in a barn with him. Bo had to break down the door to stop him from consummating a marriage she had previously refused.'

Ulrik's fists clenched instinctively as he forced himself to bite back the anger in his voice. 'I hope he was *severely* punished.'

'My father slapped him for the insult.'

Ulrik felt his face flush, and she added hastily, 'Because I clearly did not want him to touch me.' She glanced away as if embarrassed.

Did she think he feared a similar reprisal from her father?

'I would kill any man who thought to force himself on my daughter,' he replied coldly.

A heavy silence descended over the camp at his words, extinguishing all previous frivolity. Yet to Astrid they were strangely comforting. Of the two men who had ever kissed her, it proved that the one she had at least *wanted* to be kissed by was indeed the better man.

She gave a bright smile to the rest of the camp, waving aside the awkwardness with a light laugh. 'How could he? When it was my father's fault? You see, Viggo had been deep in his cups, making jests and begging for a jarl to come and claim me as his wife. Unfortunately, Bjarni took him at his word—the man has no sense of humour.' Although she refused to let it show, the words still tasted bitter in her mouth. Viggo had all but given the man permission to rape her, and she had been told to laugh it off as a joke.

Her father's reaction had not been the only cruelty, as Bjarni's betrayal had killed any hope she might have had for a romantic relationship—she had wanted someone who would view her as an equal and who would accept her ways.

Bjarni had seemed her greatest hope. He had spoken and treated her like a friend…she had even trusted him enough to follow him into the barn like a willing sacrifice. To think that if he had only been a little more patient, she might have allowed him to court her anyway. Thankfully, she had seen his true heart before it was too late. It was the only thing from that night that she was grateful for.

'Your father should never have said that.' It was a simple statement, and yet Ulrik could easily be beaten to death for speaking ill of the King. Astrid glanced around her and saw young Frida listening to the conversation with wide eyes.

Was he concerned for his daughter's safety?

That would make more sense than his being angry on her behalf.

'Please do not worry. It was a misunderstanding, nothing more. I doubt such a thing would ever happen again. But, if you are concerned for Frida, then I will ask my mother to have her as one of her companions during the festivities. She will ensure she is safe.'

'And who will ensure your safety, Princess?'

She would have liked to say that she could look after herself, but that was not entirely true, and was something that had been made clear to her at the previous festival. Her mother had promised to keep her safe this year with men like Bo beside her.

The Queen had been so enraged by Viggo's callousness that she had forced him to sleep out in the hall with his men for a week, and their relationship, already on rocky shores, seemed to have halted completely after that. Astrid still felt guilty about it—she should have taken better precautions, and should never have gone into the barn alone with Bjarni. She had been arrogant and reckless.

'Do you have a guard?' Ulrik asked again, this time in a lower voice, as the rest of the camp had returned to talking amongst themselves. They may as well have been alone by the intensity of his gaze, it seemed to hold her so tightly.

'There's Bo…and…well, I am sure my brother and the other warriors are aware. They will take precautions.' Although, in truth, her brother was very rarely interested in anything to do with her. If anything, he seemed to find her presence an embarrassment at best. 'I will also carry one of my axes with me at all times…'

This did not seem to please Ulrik. 'I will keep an eye on you as well… And come to me if anyone makes you feel uncomfortable.'

You make me uncomfortable! she almost spat back, but as his offer was made with good intentions, it felt like poor manners to refuse, so she gave a weak smile, and went back to her meal.

Why should he even care?

If she was forced to marry another, the competition

would be over. Except she had come to know him, and he was not the kind of man to revel in a success bought with dishonour.

His voice cracked like a whip. 'Do you think me incapable?'

'No,' she said, surprised by his burst of anger.

'My leg may be lame, but I am still more than capable of knocking a young buck down if needed,' he grumbled, and she chuckled at his hurt pride. It would be so easy to tease him, and as always she was unable to resist.

Easing forward in her seat, she said in a sultry voice, 'I do not doubt it. I have seen you throw logs around as if they were twigs. I am only surprised you care enough to *want* to protect me.'

Ulrik cleared his throat, and looked to his daughter. 'Frida, I think it best if you go to stay up at the hall for a while…if the Queen accepts it.'

'She will,' Astrid interrupted with a breezy smile. 'As long as you can stand to be alone with me, Ulrik? Our teams will be taking a well-earned break for the festivities, remember?'

Ulrik's eyes widened with horror. 'Will you not be at the hall then? I would have thought…' He stopped speaking, but she could imagine what he was about to say.

'Ahh, yes, my father would have preferred that I

return to the hall. But, in the spirit of fairness, my mother has insisted that I be allowed to remain. I doubt you would pass on the time to work on your carvings alone, and I should be allowed the same opportunity.'

'I would gladly lay down my tools if it guaranteed your safety.'

She wasn't sure if it was the kindness of his words or the sincerity of his expression, but her heart turned to honey as their eyes met.

'I don't want you to do that,' she whispered, her throat suddenly dry. 'I want to stay...if you don't mind?'

A flurry of chatter drew her attention away from him. In the distance she could see her father's ship entering the fjord. She put down her bowl and stood. 'I will go greet him, and while I am at the hall I shall ask my mother about Frida. I suspect the festival will begin in the next few days.'

Ulrik stood and moved to her side, his voice low and husky. 'You are always safe with me, Princess. Never doubt it.'

For some reason his words made a shiver of longing race down her spine, and she wondered for a moment if she truly wanted to be *safe*.

Chapter Thirteen

'Are you ready for your ribs and stringers?' asked Astrid as she came to stand beside Ulrik.

'Yes,' he replied, glancing over at her own ship and the frames waiting to be fitted. It was disconcerting how evenly they were matched. Following each other, step for step. The stringers gave the hull strength, and they needed to be carefully cut and measured against the ribs and hull.

The overlapping boards of the hull meant the ribs also needed to be cut precisely, and they resembled a row of teeth, slotting neatly into the spaces created by the inside of the hull. There were a few ribs in already, but the placement of these would be key to the ship's eventual strength.

Both he and Astrid had spent much of their time ensuring they would fit exactly. But it would still be a time-consuming and heavy job to lift and fit them into place. Lastly, the longer, more difficult stringers needed to be wrapped around the outside of the hull. Each of the stringers was the length of a tree trunk, and would need several vats of tar to make the joints watertight.

Astrid nodded, and shifted on her feet from side to side, as if she was nervous—which was unusual for her. 'Perhaps we can help each other?'

That caught his attention. 'How so?'

'It would be quicker and safer if more people were used to fit the stringers. Less chance of damage, and, as we must down tools soon, would it not be better to have all our stringers fitted first before a break?'

'True.' Ulrik nodded. He had considered the same, and was surprised she would be the first to approach him regarding it.

'So, my team will help yours, if yours helps mine. Agreed?' She reached out and gripped his arm ring in a silent oath.

He stared down at her small hand encasing his arm. She wore her gloves, so thankfully he was saved from the warmth of her touch. 'Agreed.'

A cheerful smile spread across her face. 'So, are you ready?'

'You would do mine first?' He laughed. 'Surely you would want to do yours, and then pretend as if we had never spoken.'

Astrid's face dropped. 'I have given you my word.'

Guilt twisted in his stomach and he suddenly felt very sorry for his lack of belief in her. For all her previous tricks she had never broken a promise. 'I was only teasing you,' he said mildly and she gave a huff of indignation.

'Well, if we make a mistake, then at least we can avoid repeating it when we put my own in,' she replied tartly, and he smiled, pleased that he had not been entirely wrong in his judgement. She still had spirit and he would be the last person to take it from her. He was even beginning to like it—at least the days were never dull.

The morning disappeared quickly. Both crews worked hard to fit the ribs. When it was time to fit the stringers, every person in camp was needed to help attach them, using brute strength to bend the timber to their will, and clamp each piece to the hull in sections. Thankfully, Ulrik's measurements were accurate, and after a few adjustments they were hammered into place.

With relieved sighs, both crews stood back to admire their work, and have some much-needed refreshment before they started work on Astrid's ship.

However, the King's deep and booming voice interrupted them. 'Greetings! Look at that! What a magnificent dragon ship!'

Ulrik and Astrid both turned as Viggo strode over

to them with a wide grin on his face. He was admiring Ulrik's ship and hadn't even looked in the direction of Astrid's.

'Father, I thought you would be welcoming your many guests? New boats seem to be arriving at every moment,' Astrid replied stiffly, and Ulrik wondered at their turbulent relationship.

Were these the potential suitors for her, was that why she sounded bitter?

'My jarls are excited about the celebrations.' Viggo grinned, still admiring Ulrik's ship. It made Ulrik feel a little uncomfortable, considering that Astrid's was equally magnificent. 'I can see you have made good progress, Ulrik. I think now would be a good time to take a break from your hard labour.'

Astrid and Ulrik exchanged alarmed looks.

'How so?' asked Astrid suspiciously.

'Your mother will need the thralls back to help with the feasts.'

'Yes, we already know that. They will return to the hall tomorrow, and be back in twelve days' time once the feasts have ended,' Astrid replied firmly.

Viggo nodded. 'Why not begin now? Since, as you say, we have so many guests?' Then, before she could reply, he shouted, 'Put down your tools! No one is to begin work again until after the celebrations!'

Astrid stared in horror at her ribs and stringers, as

if she had been gutted like a fish. 'What? Father, no! We were about to put my frame in! At least let me do that first!'

'It can wait,' replied Viggo with a scowl.

'But what if the weather turns and warps the wood?'

Her father shook his head, and smiled at the people who were gathered around with worried expressions. 'Go, enjoy the celebrations!'

Ulrik watched as the crew reluctantly began to dissipate, and the tears in Astrid's eyes threatened to spill. 'Wait!' he bellowed, stopping the crews with a raised hand. Then with an easy smile he turned to Viggo. 'Let us finish this day evenly. Astrid and her crew helped me fit my ribs and stringers. It is only fair that we do the same. Besides… I gave my word.' He patted his arm ring casually.

Astrid's sigh of relief made Viggo's glare easier to bear.

'Fine, but nothing more than that!'

Astrid rushed away, shouting orders as she did so. Ulrik went to follow her but was stopped by Viggo's reprimand. 'A man is a fool if he does not take advantage of every opportunity on the battlefield. Next time, *accept* the gift I offer you.'

Ulrik thought carefully before answering. 'In battle, yes. But this is a competition of skill. It will be a fair test, or I will not take part in it. Glory gained through corruption reflects a weakness of character. It would make Astrid the true victor in my eyes…if not yours.'

Viggo's gaze hardened for a moment, before his face broke into a mask of affable humour. 'You are a strange man, Ulrik, but no one could question your honour.'

The King left, and under Astrid's direction the group began to work. Ulrik wasn't sure if it was the familiarity of the labour after working on his own ship, or the urgency of the King's decree, but the large group worked with impressive speed, lifting and slotting each rib smoothly into position with ease. The air was filled with the hammering of nails, and the soft creaking of clamps. The crews worked well together, seamlessly moving from one job to the next with only quiet and respectful chatter.

Ulrik looked up from his own hammering, and realised something which should have been obvious from the very beginning. These people did not view themselves as rivals.

Why should they?

They had worked alongside each other for years.

How foolish and wasteful this challenge must seem to them, and how pointless and insulting it must be for Astrid.

His eyes searched for her, and he found her standing on one of the cross braces near the prow, the smell of tar thick in the salty air. She caught him staring at her, and for once she did not frown or look away. A bright and broad smile lit up her face, one of the most genuine reflections of joy he had ever seen from her, and it stole his breath.

She called out, in a loud and cheerful voice, 'Thank you, everyone! I hope you all enjoy the midsummer festivities, whether you are with your family, or helping in the hall. I thought that when we are done here, we could have a small celebration—just for us! I have two barrels of mead in my workshop, and my mother will be sending down two hogs for roasting. Let us toast our achievements, and begin our solstice celebrations a little early! Will you feast with me?'

A cheer rang out in answer, and Ulrik smiled, understanding now why she was so well-loved by those around her. Astrid might be spoilt and mischievous at times, but she was also generous and thoughtful. She must have planned this days ago, and the kindness of including both crews and the thralls was not lost on anyone.

As the people rushed towards the campfire he made his way to the back of Astrid's workshop, and rummaged in the discarded pieces of wood until he found what he was looking for—a section taken from her keel. He had kept a piece of his aside too.

It was a habit of his to make Frida a toy, or as she had gotten older a piece of jewellery, from the cast-off wood of his keel. It meant she now had a collection of trinkets marking every ship he had built.

He would carve a gift for Astrid from her keel timber, something lucky. She deserved to have something that marked the creation of her magnificent ship, and if he were honest, he wanted to give her something to remember him by.

Astrid grinned stupidly at those around her. She knew she was drunk, but she did not care. She was surrounded by friends, and would rather be here than at her parent's hall. Her mother had insisted that she return for all meals, and to join in the celebrations. So this would be her last true night of freedom, at least until the teams came back to work.

The two barrels of mead had been drained quickly, and Astrid had begged her mother for another two, promising to wear a dress for the festivities. The benevolent Queen did not disappoint, and four barrels were rolled down to the beach shortly after the request was made.

Two of them had been specifically offered to Ulrik, who had quickly shared them out as she had. Astrid was certain her mother had heard about his earlier help in regards to her build. The Queen had eyes and ears all over the kingdom, and they whispered news in her ear like Odin's ravens.

Astrid was still a little shocked that Ulrik had shown such consideration, even though it had been the honourable thing to do, and she was not sure if she would have done the same...not at the beginning at least, but now she feared she would.

The days were long now, the sun still high in the sky despite its being well past *nattmal*. Summer was always a productive and joyous time. She had almost forgotten—what with her father's challenge—to enjoy it. She could not change her father's opinion of her, but if luck was on her side she still might win. After all, her father could not go back on his word of a fair judgement, so she still had a chance.

Thanks to Ulrik, their ships were at the same stage in the building process. The remaining weeks until the autumn blot would be spent on building up the gunwale sides, mounting the mast, sail, steering oar and figurehead. But as the most crucial parts of the structure were complete, she had allowed herself one night to enjoy her achievement.

No matter what, she was already proud of her ship, and Ulrik should feel the same. She could tell that although different in size, they were evenly matched in quality.

Thinking about her rival inevitably drew her eyes to the handsome man who sat across the fire from her.

Had she been wrong to hate him?

Probably. He wasn't to blame for what had happened, her father was, and although she loved him, she had to accept that he was the one at fault, not Ulrik.

Stumbling to her feet, she filled two horns with mead, and made her way over to where Ulrik was sitting, his figurehead's timber balanced on two stools in front of him. Unable to help her curiosity, she studied the image he had sketched upon it in charcoal.

'A beautiful woman is your idea of a monster?' Astrid asked with a chuckle as she handed him a horn.

Ulrik took it with a grateful smile that made the two spots on his cheeks dip. 'Some would argue they are the most dangerous of all creatures... But no, this lady is meant to be Hel, and this will be her beautiful side.'

Astrid tried to ignore his dimples and instead frowned at the image loosely drawn on the wood. It was an excellent sketch, there was no denying it, the strong, elegant features of a goddess perfectly drawn. 'An unusual choice. It will be difficult to blend the two sides together...' Astrid said thoughtfully.

Hel ruled the underworld of those who had died of sickness or old age. She was one of the monster children of Loki, and a terrifying sight. Split down the centre, the goddess was a pretty woman on one side, and the image of death and disease on the other.

'It is a risk. But I have seen your work, and I know I must push myself if I am to compete with your skill.'

Astrid blushed at the unexpected praise. 'Well, you have made good progress. I am sure it will be impressive.'

'What about your figurehead? What beast have you chosen?'

Astrid sighed, and for a moment she contemplated not telling him the truth, but what was the point in false confidence? She glanced over at the piece of timber that was clamped upright in front of her workshop. 'I am still waiting for inspiration.' She took a long sip of her mead, letting the sweetness wash away the worry that plagued her whenever she looked at the wood.

'It will come.' His words were gentle and oddly comforting.

'I was thinking to stay more traditional…with a serpent… but I suppose that is rather dull…'

'In your hands? I doubt it. I thought your carving on *Dragon's Breath* the most beautiful I have ever seen. Besides, serpents are preferred for a reason; they bring their owners good fortune.'

Astrid felt more flames lick at her cheeks, and she wondered if perhaps she should stop drinking. 'You are being very complimentary,' she said thoughtfully, swaying ever so slightly from side to side. 'Have I done something to please you for once?'

Ulrik cleared his throat loudly, and took a sip from his own mead before answering. 'I only speak the truth. Beauty and elegance are not where I excel. I know where my skills lie—in the shape and size of my ship.'

More heat seemed to burn her cheeks and she giggled. 'Are those your *best attributes?*'

He rolled his eyes with an exasperated laugh, and looked away. 'You are impossible.'

Unable to control herself, she was horrified when she gave a loud snort of laughter.

The usually surly Ulrik looked up with a wide, surprised grin. 'You should sit down before you fall.'

'Perhaps…' she agreed, and he shifted aside as she dropped down on the log beside him. Before she lost her confidence, she leaned in and whispered, 'Thank you for helping me earlier…with my father.'

Ulrik shrugged as if it was nothing, and she tried not to sigh wantonly as his large biceps brushed against her arm.

'I meant what I said—this should be a fair contest, or I will not take part in it.'

She rolled her horn sourly, her voice full of bitterness. 'But life is not fair.'

He nodded, all humour dying from his expression. 'You are right. So, is it not more important to be fair and honourable with each other when we can?'

Her eyes met his and she found herself tilting closer. He raised his hand and gripped her shoulder to stop her from falling into his lap.

How she wished he would kiss her again.

She had thought of little else for weeks!

As if a dam had broken inside of her, her words came out in a sudden rush. 'I am sorry for before, for the *elves*...the games and tricks I played. In truth, I was afraid.'

'Of losing?'

'No.' She shook her head, immediately regretting it when the world began to spin. 'No... I am afraid of this life ending.' She threw out her arms wide, one hand thudding into his chest. 'Here I am free to be myself. My life has beauty and purpose. I have friends and a home. But if I lose the contest, all of that will end.' She pulled her arms back in to wrap around herself. 'If I am not good enough to call myself master builder then so be it. I will understand and not hold you to blame for the changes it will bring. But I will still mourn this life. I doubt I will taste such freedom again.'

'Not all men are trolls. You may find you like married life...maybe even more so than this.'

She scoffed at his words. 'I want to carve! You think a jarl's son would be happy for me to do that?'

'Family, children...they all give life greater meaning. You could find happiness down another path.'

She shook her head until her ears rang. 'You do not understand.'

'Perhaps not...this craft has always been a livelihood to me. Without it, I cannot provide for my daughter. You are lucky to have a father who can offer you the best of everything. Even if I worked every day of my life without rest, I could not offer Frida the same.'

'I imagine Frida does not want that either. Most of my life I have only wanted one thing...for my father to accept me. To value what I value, and take pride in my work. But he only sees me as a broodmare to be bartered and sold to whoever suits his own ambitions.'

'Perhaps he just wants the best for you—for you to be settled and provided for?'

'I am sure that is what you want for Frida. But I do not think my father and you have much in common. You love your daughter.'

'Your father loves you,' he said firmly, his rough hand dropping to cover hers.

'Sometimes I am not so certain. How can you love something that you so thoroughly dislike?'

Her words hung heavy in the air, and she found herself staring into his face and knowing with absolute certainty that she did not, and could not, hate Ulrik.

'Astrid,' he whispered, and her name on his tongue overflowed with compassion.

Tugging her hand away, she waved dramatically towards the hall. 'That is why so many jarls are here! He is already gathering up the wolves. Mark my words! He will cut loose the weak from the pack, and only the strongest will return for the autumn blot. If I lose, they will be the final suitors I have to choose from, ready and waiting. My father plans everything to benefit only himself. I wouldn't be surprised if he planned to have me wedded and bedded before the first snow falls.'

'You can still say no. You *are* a princess.'

Astrid stared at him in disbelief. 'I *have* said no, for *years!*'

Ulrik suddenly looked miserable, and she patted his arm in what she hoped was a soothing gesture, although her palm stung afterwards, so she suspected it was a little harder than she had intended. 'I do not say this to make you feel bad. I know this is not what you wished for either.' Sighing, she lifted her horn towards him. 'I wish you and your daughter well. If I win, you may remain and join my team.'

Ulrik chuckled, but raised his horn. 'I will be the master or I shall leave. But I thank you for the offer. Would you accept a position beneath me?'

Astrid burst into a fit of giggles, and Ulrik rolled his eyes. 'If I was made master builder!'

Astrid shook her head. 'No. My father would never accept that.'

He nodded. 'Because I am only a freeman. Not a jarl or a king. I have no right to give orders to a princess.'

'Yes, there is that.' Resting her head against his shoulder, she added, 'I wish you well with your figurehead. I think it will be most impressive.'

'Thank you, Princess.'

Later, Astrid was vaguely aware of Ulrik carrying her to her bed. She wrapped her wrists around his neck and hugged him close. As he raised himself up, he had to untangle himself from her, and she grumbled at the loss of his body.

'Ulrik?' she asked, snuggling down into her luxurious bedding with a happy sigh.

'Yes, Princess?'

'Are you carving Hel for your wife?'

There was a long pause before he answered, and he

sat down on the bed beside her. 'In a way… In hon-
ouring Hel, I also pay respect to my wife.'

'How did she die?'

'She fell while trying to fix our roof.'

Astrid gripped his hand and gave it a gentle
squeeze. 'I am sorry. You must miss her terribly.'

He shook his head. 'I did. But over the years the
pain has dulled. I still wish to remember her though,
for Frida's sake.'

Astrid nodded. 'Of course you do.' She rolled onto
her side, and buried her head in her pillow before mur-
muring, 'I wish someone loved me like that.'

He was gone when she awoke the next morning,
and she hoped he hadn't heard her last words.

Chapter Fourteen

'You look beautiful!' her mother exclaimed, and Astrid shook out the ice-blue dress with a flick of her wrists.

She did not feel beautiful, she felt exposed and awkward, as if she were a little girl once more forced into clothing that made her itch. 'It was wasteful to make me a new gown—I will probably only wear it a few times.'

'You have so few dresses, Astrid! And I wanted no excuse for you to go back on your word.'

Astrid frowned at her mother, who was seated on a silk-covered chair, surrounded by her favourite ladies, as well as the wives, daughters, and sisters of the visiting jarls. Frida was there too, staring at the wealth and extravagant gowns around her in awe, her delicate hand crunching the wool of her apron nervously.

Inga had accepted Ulrik's daughter into her household gladly, treating her with as much respect as she did any of the high-status women. Astrid hoped the others would do the same. In her experience, the ladies of powerful men could be vicious, especially her sisters.

'Come help me with the flower garlands,' urged her mother, and Astrid sat beside her feet on one of the cushions and began to weave a crown of flowers from the fragrant piles stacked high on the low table in front of them.

Her mother had a large flower garden devoted to growing blooms for the spring and summer festivals. This year seemed to have been a particularly impressive harvest. Astrid eased back against her mother's legs and began to work. Normally she did not mind this task—it had always been one of the few feminine crafts she enjoyed. But today there was a strange coolness in the air that bothered her like a fly buzzing in her ear.

'Tell me, how is the build going?' asked her mother pleasantly.

Astrid nodded. 'We are making good progress, and matching Ulrik's pace. Although he has begun work on his figurehead already. When I am not helping with the festival, am I still allowed to carve at the workshops?'

'If you must, but I do not approve of your sleeping there all alone.'

Astrid sighed with relief. Her mother may not approve of her decision, but at least she would support it. Rather than bait her further, she decided to concentrate on weaving some delicate alpine berry flowers, and said lightly, 'It is too crowded here. Ulrik is only nextdoor, and Bo can walk me to and from the festivities—his smithy is not far, and he is such a good man, so trustworthy.' She glanced at Skadi—the woman Bo wished to court—and was pleased when she saw the young woman blush prettily.

Bodil leaned forward, her dark red hair pouring over her shoulder like Frankish wine. 'And…tell me about Ulrik. When we first met him, he was as hairy as a bear, but I hear his looks have improved considerably since?'

Frida flinched, and a wave of anger swept through Astrid, even though she had said something similar herself—she couldn't stomach her sister's snide criticism. 'A hairy bear? He is a master boat-builder and a freeman. Is that how you speak of the man who saved our father's life?'

Bodil and Liv exchanged a meaningful look. Slyly Liv asked, 'I am surprised *you* speak so well of him, sister. Is he not your rival?'

'I can still appreciate his valued position and skill.' Astrid huffed, bruising a bunch of pink and white flowers as she stuffed them into the hazel crown.

'*Valued position and skill?*' Bodil crowed. 'How about his handsome face? I have heard he is quite the sight, and who would have thought such a man existed under all that hair?'

'Have some respect—his daughter is present!'

'Oh, but we are not saying anything unkind, are we...? What is your name, girl?' Bodil turned to Frida expectantly. Frida bobbed her head politely and mumbled her name.

Liv sighed lazily, her smile full of cunning. 'I am so thirsty. Bring me some ale, girl.'

Frida jumped to her knees obediently.

'Frida, do not move!' snapped Astrid, and Frida hesitated like a frightened deer. Glaring at her sister, she snarled, 'She is not one of your thralls to command. She is a free woman!'

'Barely... I have cows with better lineage!' Liv chuckled wickedly. 'Anyway, why such concern for a rival's child?'

Queen Inga quickly raised a hand to one of her thralls, and gave both her daughters a look of warning. 'Please can you bring us some refreshments? Astrid is right. Frida is an honoured guest. The King invited her father here especially. *And, Liv,* remember your manners when speaking to my guests—you sound far too proud!'

Frida quietly lowered herself back into a sitting

position, but she looked terrified, particularly when Liv gave her a haughty look of disdain. Astrid sat on her hands to stop herself from scratching out her sister's eyes.

But her sister did not care—she was a huntress, who preyed on gossip and others' humiliation like a wolf. 'Why are you so offended, Astrid? *Unless...*' She paused and exchanged a knowing look with her other sibling.

Bodil shook her head as if amazed. 'Honestly, I did not believe it...until now!'

The Queen interrupted them with barely concealed irritation. 'Believe what?'

'Has a man finally caught your interest, sister?' asked Liv, and then with a snort of laughter, she added, 'I should have known you would pick someone so deeply inappropriate to lust after!'

Her sisters fell against each other, cackling with amusement, and Astrid tried her best to mask her embarrassment. 'Have you both lost your minds, or are your married lives so dull that you must make up stupid lies for your own amusement?'

They stopped laughing and both scowled at her. Liv was the first to bite back. 'One of the thralls saw you being carried to your bed by Ulrik last night. So, do not act all innocent with me, *little sister!*'

The Queen's face flushed pink. '*What?* Why am I only hearing of this now?'

The crown in Astrid's hands became twisted and bent. Ulrik's life hung in the balance…a wrong word could devastate his reputation and his place here. Poor Frida looked as if she was going to faint, and Brenna's gaze flew away from her guiltily.

Astrid laughed loudly, trying to hide her fear. 'It was nothing! I had too much to drink! Ulrik merely helped me to my bed! Ask anyone—he returned to the feast straight after, didn't he, Frida?' In answer, Frida nodded rapidly, and Astrid wagged her finger at her sisters as if they were naughty children. 'You two have such wild imaginations…maybe you should find something better to do with your time. Gossiping is such a vulgar pastime.'

Astrid glanced at Brenna, and she could tell the woman felt bad for what she had done. She decided not to be angry at the thrall—she could imagine the pestering and bullying her sisters would have done to her, and it only made her feel sorry for her.

Liv's anger whipped out like a lash. 'He may have returned straight after, but they said your arms were wrapped around his neck like weeds! Really, Astrid, you could have your pick of any man, and you choose him? Father is right! It is long past time you were plucked!'

Astrid did not have time to think, she merely reacted, throwing the warped crown straight at Liv's head. It smacked her square in the nose, snapping the woman's head back, before flopping into her lap.

There was a moment of silence, and then Liv's indignant scream pierced the hall. Sweeping up a bunch of flowers into her fists, her sister threw herself across the table and began hitting Astrid wildly with them. In retaliation, Astrid picked up some hazel and began to whip it against her sister's backside, while grabbing at her hair.

Through the roar of fury, she dimly heard her mother beseeching them to stop, and then hands grabbed at them and pulled them apart.

Liv hissed like a wild cat, and Astrid did the same. Bodil was howling with laughter, while the rest of the women gasped out horrified exclamations, or grunted as they tried to restrain the two sisters.

'Enough!' shouted the Queen, and everyone fell silent. 'We have much to do in preparation for the opening celebration tonight. I suggest we all work in *silence* to ensure it is done in time. The next person to disrupt our work will spend the rest of the day locked in a sea chest, regardless of who they are!'

Astrid and Liv shrugged out of their captors' hold and gave a begrudging nod to the Queen, their hair in disarray and still panting from exertion. When they sat back down they glowered at each other across the scattered petals and broken flower stems.

Ulrik made his way with the rest of the crowd up the mountainside.

At the head of the procession was the royal family surrounded by their elite warriors, who carried their banners, wreaths, and a giant wooden wheel. Later it would be lit and rolled into the sea, symbolising the death of the summer sun, but that would be at the end of the feasting. Today, only the bonfire was to be lit, and the wheel would remain a safe distance away, wreathed in flowers.

Drums began to beat, and the people started to sing in harmony, their voices soaring joyfully into the clear sky above.

It was one of the old songs, loved and familiar to every member of Viggo's kingdom—except Ulrik. They walked in a long procession up the well-trodden path and around the hillside, their destination the huge bonfire, ready and waiting on the cliff that overlooked the fjord.

The royal family walked at the head of the crowd, the King's respected warriors beside them. Then there were the jarls and their loved ones, the Queen's ladies and relatives. Most wore crowns of flowers, while men had the sacred nine herbs pinned to their tunics.

Important freemen walked behind them, followed by people like himself, and then finally the thralls.

A familiar figure wove downstream towards Ulrik and he called out to her, 'Frida, what are you doing here? Should you not be with the Queen and her household?'

His daughter rushed towards him and enveloped him in a fierce embrace that forced him to shift his weight to stand firm.

'I wanted to be with you. At least for the ceremony,' she mumbled, although she looked a little pale and frightened.

'Are you well?'

Frida nodded, and then after glancing behind them she said, 'We should hurry—we do not want to lose our place.'

He frowned, realising that a few of the thralls were waiting for them to proceed, and with a grateful nod he walked forward, draping a protective arm around Frida's shoulders. 'Did something happen? It is not like you to care about rank.'

Frankly, they had never needed to care in the past. Aalborg had been so chaotic in structure, with people always coming and going, both foreign and local traders, as well as many thralls. So their place in society had made no difference, because people rarely stayed long enough to know.

Frida gathered her cloak around her, as if she were cold. 'I did not realise how important it was until now.'

He frowned at that, but spoke in a gentle tone, hoping to draw more from her. 'What happened?'

Frida sighed. 'Astrid got into trouble because of us.'

'How so?'

Frida's voice became hushed, and he had to lean down to hear her better over the singing and drums. 'The Princess Liv…she ordered me to bring her ale, and Astrid told her I was not a thrall to do her bidding.'

Ulrik rolled his eyes, and begged Odin for patience. 'If a princess asks you to do something, you should do it.'

'Astrid told me not to…and she is a princess too!'

'I can see how that must have confused you. What happened then?'

Frida looked up at him with tears in her eyes, and he wanted to strangle Astrid for putting her in such a terrible position. 'They fought…*really* fought; it was awful…'

'That is not your fault. Sisters fight sometimes, even princesses.'

She remained silent, as if considering his words with great thought.

'Was there something else?' he prodded, suspecting there was more to it than what had been said. But Frida shook her head and began to sing along with the crowd.

As they reached the clifftop a hazy light filled the sky: the midnight sun. It was as if the Queen had gathered every flower of the world, so abundant were they in the crowns and bouquets of the people, as well as the decorations. Lush, greenery-covered poles stood in a circle on the clifftop. Intricately woven wreaths hung from them, depicting the runes of the gods and goddesses in summer blooms.

It was the Queen's honour to light the bonfire, and she wore a resplendent gown in gold, with a matching silk-trimmed cloak, and an elaborate golden crown. The King's clothing and crown matched hers, whilst their children wore blue with silver crowns.

His eyes immediately sought out Astrid, and his chest tightened when he saw her. He had never seen her in a dress before, and if anything, it only sharpened her regal beauty. The silver crown sat upon her unbound hair, which flowed down her shoulders in a waterfall of rich, earthy colours. Her bright blue eyes swept over the expectant crowd with an uninterested expression. Only Astrid would be bored at such an important occasion, and it almost made him laugh.

The Queen raised her hand and the music stopped, a hush falling over the crowd. 'Tonight, we pray to

Odin, Frey and Freya. Let our harvests be plentiful and our winter short.' She approached the bonfire. It towered over her, as tall as the great hall and as wide as two barn doors. 'We make this offering to you, so that you might know our love and devotion.'

Tar-covered barrels filled with straw were placed amongst the timber, as well as carvings of the gods that were almost as tall as a man. Ulrik recognised Astrid's hand in the beautiful lines, and thought it a shame that such excellent work would be turned to ash. But that was the point of offerings, and new ones would be carved in the autumn to protect them throughout the winter.

The King came to stand beside his wife, and he handed her a torch. The drums began to beat and the crowd began to sing. The Queen lit a barrel, and then moved to stand with her family. Together they watched as the bonfire in front of them was quickly engulfed in flames.

Astrid's silks shone in the firelight and the world seemed to dim around her. Ulrik's heart squeezed painfully when he realised how far away Astrid was from him, in every way.

He wanted her, but could never have her. They were too far removed from one another in status, ambition, and in duty.

Astrid was too rash in her actions, and seemed

completely unaware of the position she had put Frida in. She may not follow the rules of society herself, but she had to learn that those of lower rank had to.

It was a timely reminder to himself about his own behaviour. Last night he had wanted to kiss her, and the fact that she was so obviously drunk had been the only thing to stop him.

The crowd began to dance, and Frida took his hand. Leading him in a circle around the fire. Slower, of course, because of his leg. Others did the same, and each band of people reflected a different class, from the jarls in the centre out to the thralls behind him.

He knew his place.

Chapter Fifteen

The hall was so filled with the sound of voices that if you placed your hand against the timber beams you could feel them. Children and dogs ran between the tables, some people danced to the music, while others flirted in the darkened corners—in another kind of dance.

Astrid's sisters and their husbands sat on the King and Queen's feasting table, while everyone else sat on rows of benches up and down the hall. Light filled the space from the fires and torches as well as from the open shutters that let in the milky midnight sun. Her brother played Tafl with one of her father's men, and the jarls were gathered around congratulating young Viggo on each of his moves. At least her younger brother had the good sense to ignore them.

Everyone had eaten their fill of the sumptuous feast offered, but there would be more to come. Her mother had emptied an entire farm's worth of livestock, grain, and vegetables to feed her guests. It was a sign of generosity from their ruler, but also a means to strengthen loyalty. The extravagance was nothing to a leader who regularly brought home ships filled with plunder. No one would question who ruled here and why.

Her father came to stand beside her. 'Jarl Gunnar is the latest man to swear his sword to me. Should I introduce you?'

Astrid sighed. 'Why?'

'His lands are further south and filled with oak.'

She smoothed her hands down her gown, and the unfamiliar clothing felt odd, especially the crotchless leggings she wore beneath. It made it easier for women to relieve themselves, but she found it strange after wearing trousers for so long. 'I see. Does he require a master shipbuilder, then?'

Her father scowled at her deliberate misunderstanding. 'No.'

'Then there is no reason for us to speak.'

She got up and began to walk away, but her father's firm hand stopped her. 'I would pay more interest regarding the men here tonight. If you do not win the challenge, one of them will become your husband. I would know which one suits you best.'

Astrid's fists clenched at her sides and she faced her father with a bitter glare. 'None of them!'

'Be reasonable, Astrid. All I want is for you to be

happy and well settled, so at least take some time to consider them—it is for your own benefit.'

It reminded her of what Ulrik had once said, and she shook her head. 'Why must I? Why not leave me as I am? I am happy *and* settled. I want to remain unmarried and stay here. What is so wrong with that? Mother—'

The mention of Inga seemed to anger Viggo, and he interrupted her. 'You should not live your life according to what your mother wants. I know that she encourages you in this madness.'

'Madness? Because I do not wish to marry someone I have no feelings for?'

'Then go, speak with the jarls! Allow yourself time to develop *feelings* for one of them. But you will not—you have never even tried to find a match! What is to become of you when I am gone? Your sisters have their own families, and young Viggo will have his. But what of you? Who will protect you when he is away?'

'Who has protected Mother?' Astrid said with a sigh. 'She has ruled quite happily in your absence, Father. We are not useless. Who do you think has looked after us all these years?'

A hard look entered her father's eyes and he stepped closer. '*My name!* That is what has protected you *and* your mother in my absence! The blood I have spilled on countless battlefields while you sat at home playing with pieces of wood. Your mother was once a queen in her own right, but do you know why she *really* married me? Because I could keep her safe! Think on that the next time you wish to live a life alone. Your position, even the freedom you have come to expect as your due, is all won from the blood of many! And when I am gone, no one will care that you were once a princess. If young Viggo fails to secure the kingdom they will seek out his relatives, his mother and anyone else unprotected and they will slaughter them. As I have done to my enemies in the past! I thought last summer you might have realised it…how quickly men turn into beasts when they believe nothing can stop them. I do not offer you these men for my own advantage—but for your protection.'

He left her then, and Astrid felt as if the marrow in her bones had frozen solid. Her eyes found her mother staring back at her, and there was a sad look in her eyes, as if she knew the harsh truth Astrid had learned.

Had her father deliberately encouraged Bjarni to teach her a lesson?

Someone jostled her by mistake, and she suddenly felt suffocated in the throng of people. The hall was bursting at the seams, and the air felt hot and damp. Her mother's bundles of dried flowers hung from the rafters, perfuming the air, but even those were not enough to mask the stench of so many people.

Then she saw Bjarni walking towards her from the group of jarls, and she wanted to retch. The memory of his attempt last summer to force himself upon her still made her skin crawl. She avoided his eyes and quickly slipped away through the crowd, weaving her way towards the open doors. From the heavy and determined look he had given her, she would wager he had not forgotten his ambition to wed her. She only prayed her father had not given him permission for a second time.

It was insulting to think that her father still welcomed him to their hall after what he had done. Even worse, to think that it had been deliberate. She had found some small comfort in thinking that he had only encouraged the man by mistake…but what if it had been deliberate?

Bjarni had only been slapped, and when her mother had complained about the lack of serious punishment, Viggo had said, '*Did I not do similar to win your hand?*'

It made Astrid wonder about her parents' strange relationship. She had always thought that her father had courted Inga until she had fallen in love with him. But now she wondered if the beginning of their marriage had not been as romantic as she had first imagined. However, things must have changed because even Inga admitted that she had loved him once… It was truly odd.

Thinking back to the attack, she was grateful she had not been seriously hurt—or worse, trapped in an unwanted union. But those helpless moments had still felt like an eternity. His hands clawing at her breasts, the press of his ale-covered lips against hers… She had never been so angry or so frightened in her entire life. Thankfully, Bo had broken down the door well before it had gone too far.

She breathed a sigh of relief as she walked out of the hall and into the fresh air. But then a shadow fell over her, and she instinctively reached for her axe. To her relief, it was Ulrik, not Bjarni, and her hand drifted away from her belt.

She had not seen him during the lighting ceremony, and had only spotted him occasionally during the feast. But that was because she had to appear the dutiful daughter beside her family. She hated being away from her friends, but even her mother expected her to follow tradition at important celebrations.

'The blond man with the scar down the left side of his face—was that Jarl Bjarni, the man who attacked you before?' he asked quietly, and she was surprised he would use such words. If Bjarni heard he could challenge him for questioning his honour—the fact that he had no honour to start with meant nothing.

'Yes, how did you guess?'

Ulrik glared back towards the hall, but thankfully Bjarni had not followed them outside. 'I do not like the way he looks at you. It is…too possessive.'

A shiver ran down her spine, but not from fear. It was the awareness that there was only one man she wished to be possessed by, and he had already rejected her…twice.

'Well, he does not possess me; no one does!' she snapped.

To her disappointment Ulrik did not argue with her, only nodded, and sipped from the horn in his hand.

Why did she want him to argue with her? What had she expected? That he would shout loud enough for all to hear that she was his woman?

The revellers were not restricted to the inside of the hall. Outside thralls and ordinary folk drank and danced, sitting on barrels and benches they had pulled out from their homes.

Skadi broke off from the circle of dancing women and rushed to her side. 'Astrid! Will you come and dance with us?' she asked, a little breathless. Her eyes were bright with mead, her blonde hair sweeping around her face in messy braids.

Astrid nodded and joined the group with a smile,

allowing herself to be tugged into position by Skadi. She had always liked the woman, even more so now that she knew she had accepted Bo. He had always been a good judge of character.

They began to twirl and spin, hands locked together. In no time, Astrid was giggling uncontrollably as their pace and wild movements intensified.

During a pause in the music, Skadi gasped with a lop-sided grin, 'Bo has asked to marry me!'

Astrid gave her a quick hug. 'Congratulations—I am sure you will be very happy with him!'

Skadi nodded, with a giggle that twisted into a hiccup. 'Thank you! I am so happy. I was scared he would never ask me, and now I am the happiest woman alive! *Oh, Astrid,*' she cried, 'you are too pretty to toil away as a boat-builder.'

Astrid knew Skadi only meant well—she was one of her mother's treasured servants, and spent her days on tapestries or embroidery and not hard physical labour. So she protested, 'It is what I love!' Although she was so out of breath by this point, she could hardly speak the words.

Skadi twirled with a giggle. 'There are other things to love…'

Astrid laughed. 'I am sure there are.'

The humour died in her throat as she remembered her searing kiss with Ulrik, an embrace that had made her forget the horrible touches of Bjarni. The press of Ulrik's mouth tormented her in a much sweeter way, and still lingered in her dreams. Was that the only taste of pleasure she would have?

For a wild moment she wondered what would happen if she sought him out tonight. Frida was with her mother, so he would be home alone.

Skadi gasped as Bo's arms wrapped around her and plucked her from the dance. 'The King has granted our request to marry. We can have the ceremony during the festival, whenever you want!' he said, and Skadi squealed with delight, pressing quick kisses to both his cheeks. Bo blushed, then swung her onto his shoulder and strode away to his smithy with her. Nobody blinked—they were used to such things during the feasts, and it was not as if Skadi minded…she was still giggling furiously even as he carried her away.

It was no wonder so many babes came after the midsummer festival. The long days seemed to encourage romance. For once, Astrid was jealous of another woman. Not because of Bo, of course, but for the easy choices she could make. If Skadi spent that night with the man she loved, even before she was officially married, no one would care.

Astrid swayed on her feet; she was exhausted. To the north, the sky had turned dark blue, and to the south she could see the first rays of a new sunrise.

Ulrik came to stand beside her. 'I am going home now. Shall we walk together?'

She gave a grateful nod. 'If you do not mind.'

She trusted Ulrik to keep her safe, as she would have trusted Bo or any of the other boat-builders.

How strange that she would trust the one man she was meant to hate!

But that emotion had been twisting and changing for weeks, and, like a butterfly breaking free from its chrysalis, what emerged was something entirely new.

'Why should I mind?' He offered her his arm and she took it.

They walked towards the twilight. 'Your summer days really are never-ending this far north. I did not believe it until I saw it for myself,' Ulrik said.

'Did they not have them where you come from? I never asked where you used to live, did I?'

'Aalborg.' He shook his head. 'I am a Dane. The days are still long in the summer, but nothing like this.'

'I hear the winters are gentler further south.'

'That is what they say. I will have to wait and see before I can tell you for certain.'

'The days become very short here, and they are bitterly cold. The snow is so thick and heavy that sometimes we do not even leave our homes for days. That is why the light festivals are so important.'

Ulrik stopped walking and looked out at the fjord. 'It is beautiful, though. I imagine it will be the same no matter the time of year.'

Astrid paused, allowing herself a moment to admire the scenery, as well as the man—rarely did she find such an opportunity, as normally when they spoke together those perceptive blue eyes missed nothing. 'It is.'

He looked towards her then. 'I cannot deny that I wish to stay here.'

'Astrid!' called a voice from behind them, and Ulrik's smile vanished.

They turned to see Bjarni striding down the beach towards them, and Astrid groaned.

'May I speak with you?' he asked Astrid when he joined them.

'If you must, Jarl Bjarni,' she answered stiffly.

Ulrik gave the man a cool glare, before turning to Astrid. 'I will wait there, Princess.' He pointed towards a large boulder less than fifty paces away, but as he walked past Bjarni he deliberately placed his hand on top of the axe that hung from his belt.

'Speak quickly. I do not wish to be approached by you again,' Astrid said, looking out across the water and trying her best not to show her revulsion. She did not want her father blaming her for a quarrel between them.

'I wished to apologise. For my behaviour last summer. Please know that I would never have harmed you.' He chuckled at the end, but she did not join in the laughter, and it died quickly.

Turning towards him, she said, 'You did harm me.' His eyes widened with alarm. 'You kissed me without my permission. You held me captive.'

'It was only for a moment—you make it seem far worse than it was!' he grumbled, looking away. He swallowed deeply when he saw Ulrik glaring at him. 'It was barely any time at all. I misunderstood your father, and had had far too much ale that night. Please, take pity on me and forgive me my youthful exuberance. I, too, was a captive...a captive of your beauty. Astrid, you would make me a perfect wife. Let us begin again, and I will prove it to you.'

His smile made her nauseous, but as he was a jarl she had to show him respect, especially as he had now personally apologised to her. 'I will forgive you this once. For the good of the kingdom.'

'Ahh, Astrid, I knew you would be gracious. Thank you!'

She wanted to pick him up and throw him in the sea—he did not deserve her forgiveness. Instead she gave him one of her mother's haughty and dismissive looks. If he did not fear the woman, at least let him fear her status. 'I am a princess, Bjarni, and, though you are a jarl, I would never consider you for a husband. I wish you well, but do not look to me when you search for a wife.'

Astrid walked away towards Ulrik, who must have heard everything and had a grim countenance. She did not bother to look back and see what Bjarni thought of her words.

In silence she and Ulrik approached the workshops, and when she turned to say goodnight she realised he was already walking to his own home without even saying a farewell.

'Goodnight,' she said quietly with a frown, wondering what had turned him into a stranger so suddenly. Did he think she had exaggerated the attack by Bjarni? Everyone else apart from her mother and close friends seemed to have thought so.

She bolted her door, lit the fire, and began to prepare for bed, telling herself that Ulrik's opinion did not matter.

A short time later there was a rustling sound outside her door. Picking up a kitchen knife and one of her axes, she made her way to the door. Through the gaps in the wood she could see a dark shadow.

'Bjarni, if that is you…!' Irritation and fear raced up her spine, and she could feel her heart hammering in her chest.

'It is Ulrik!' came a quick reply, and she threw aside the bolt to open the door.

Huddled on the ground and wrapped in a blanket sat Ulrik.

'What are you doing?' she asked, bewildered.

He looked up at her, his voice husky and firm. 'I did not like how Jarl Bjarni spoke to you.'

'And so you have decided to spend the night against my door?'

From the blanket he withdrew a battleaxe, the kind that could fell a horse and rider in one swing. 'He is a jarl. I cannot beat him for his words. But here I can protect you. Should he dare darken your door, I will take his head.'

Astrid stared at the savage-looking weapon, and did not doubt his words. 'Come inside!' she hissed, after regaining her senses, and she stepped aside to gesture him in. The fact he cared enough to guard her made her feel dizzy.

'I am fine here.'

'Come inside if you wish to protect me. At least then you will be comfortable.'

He looked genuinely horrified by her offer. 'I have no right…'

'Get in here, before anyone sees you…or me!' she exclaimed, pointing down at the fact she was only wearing her linen shift.

Ulrik braced his arms against the timber frame of the door and raised himself up. As usual the sight gave her butterflies. The strength of his upper body to haul himself up without relying on his knees was astounding, as was the intensity of his blue eyes as they rose to loom over her.

She took a step back, but he didn't follow.

'It is best if I stay outside. Especially if you are worried about others seeing us together.'

'I am worried they will see you curled up at my door like a lonely dog. Not that they will see us together.'

Ulrik frowned. 'I just witnessed you turn down a *jarl* because he was not worthy of you. Imagine the outrage if I was to be found in your bed chamber?'

Anger flared to life, and she snapped, 'Bjarni is *not* worthy of me, and never will be! You think because he is a jarl, he is somehow better than you? His position was given by birth, and I would not be surprised if he lost it soon—I wager that is why he *really* wants me, to strengthen his own standing with my father. He lacks conviction, and talks like a whiny child. I would never consider him my equal, and neither should you.'

'I behaved just as he did…'

'What are you talking about?'

Ulrik lowered his eyes and stared at his feet glumly. 'We both kissed you when we should not have.'

He remained outside the doorway, and with one sharp tug she grabbed his tunic and dragged him inside. Once he was in, she wasted no time in slamming the door and pushing him back against it. At any moment he could easily have stopped her, but he did not, and his broad shoulders thudded against the wooden door, shaking the dust from the timbers without complaint.

She stepped forward, the light from the fire flickering across his handsome face as he watched her move. 'I *wanted* you to kiss me,' she said softly, closing the distance between them.

'I should not have…'

She cupped his jaw in her hand, her thumb brushing on the spot where his dimple would be—if he were smiling, which he was not. Then she pressed her lips softly against his. Motionless he stared at her, and she took a step back, suddenly regretting the rashness of her actions, but unable to help herself. 'This time, I was the one to kiss you. So there is no question about who is to blame.'

'I doubt your father would agree.'

'There are some things my father has no say in, and who I choose to kiss is one of them.' She took a deep breath. 'I want you, Ulrik. And, no matter who wins, this summer will be the last chance for me to do as I wish. Either you will have to leave, or my father will marry me to a man like Bjarni. We will probably never see each other again. Not as equals anyway.'

And if they were going to part ways, she wanted to experience this once with someone she admired and wanted in her bed.

'Astrid...' Her name sounded rough on his lips, like a broken oath.

'Stay with me tonight. Let me choose one thing for myself. Let me choose...*you*.'

Chapter Sixteen

Ulrik's heart beat so hard, it was as if it were about to burst out of his chest. He couldn't believe Astrid had offered herself to him, and he sucked in a breath to try and steady himself. 'This is madness,' he gasped, but he was already reaching to touch her face, intoxicated by her in every way. He wanted to be reckless, to abandon all reason and follow his own desires.

He wanted to live as Astrid lived, without thought to the consequences of his actions. To be so wrapped up in the emotions of the moment that all worries were cast into distant memory.

She was free to live like that…*at least until autumn*. His stomach flipped, knowing that soon everything would change for them, and it wouldn't be for the better. Because life *was* unfair, and for once he refused to accept it.

Watching Bjarni's snivelling apology seemed to have affected him in more ways than one. Not only had he been disgusted by the man's lack of honour and respect, but he had also hated the mere sight of him speaking to Astrid.

And if Bjarni considered himself a good match for her, he didn't deserve her. No man did—not even himself. But she should at least have a choice in the matter. At the feast, Ulrik had overheard too many jarls muttering about Astrid as if she were a piece of jewellery, something pretty and valuable, but without soul. Not one of them cared about her bravery, kindness, mischievousness, or her talent. They cared only for her name and status. They talked about her character as if it were a flaw that needed to be reworked and polished. It was sad that they were blind to her true beauty, and wanted to scratch out the very heart of her.

They did not appreciate her as he did, and he wanted more than anything to show Astrid that she was worth more than any of those men deserved.

'Just once,' she begged, pressing her lips against the pulse of his neck. 'That is all I ask, to experience at least once what I will never have otherwise.'

The rein on his self-control snapped, and he fumbled as he placed his battleaxe against the door to bar it. Then he reached for her, her eyes drowsy with desire as he cupped her face.

'You are not drunk?' he asked, and she shook her head.

'I learnt my lesson.' She pressed her forehead against his, and with trembling lips shared his air. She tugged him further into the room, as if afraid to let go of him.

Smiling, he pulled away a little to see her face better. 'You are rather sweet when you are drunk.'

She tilted her head with a playful pout, and he kissed her with a chuckle.

'I wanted you to kiss me again,' she confessed, wrapping her arms around his neck.

All amusement flew from his mind as he surrendered to their desires. He could not deny her anything. Pressing his lips against hers, she opened for him, encouraging him to taste her more deeply. Lust raced through his veins. She was so soft and warm, full of life and fire.

Once could never be enough, but it had to be.

They moved towards the bed, their tongues sliding against one another with increasing urgency. The arguments, bickering and desire that had been building between them from the first day they met seemed to have finally overwhelmed them. Never had he felt such mindless passion, and it shook him to his core.

'There is no need to rush,' he whispered, even though, truth be told, he was worried he would be the one rushing her. 'The days are endless here, remember.'

Astrid clawed at his clothes, and he knelt on the bed to undo his belt, dropping it on the floor, the leather sighing as it fell. Next he cupped her face, and she leant in to the caress, closing her eyes softly.

Holding his breath, he waited for her to reject him, to realise the madness of this moment and push him away, but instead she lay down, and stared up at him expectantly. His heart unravelled and he sank down by her side, not wishing to crush her.

They kissed, her body tilted towards him, eager for his touch, and he refused to disappoint her. Gripping her lower back, he tugged her close. Gasping against her mouth as their hips met, he leaned over and pressed her into the blankets and furs, unable to resist pushing the hardness of his body against hers.

If this was only going to be once, then he would make sure that they both remembered it forever.

Astrid moaned as the delicious weight of Ulrik stole the breath from her body.

Was this really going to happen?

Over the years she had presumed that, as she did not wish to marry, this aspect of life would be forbidden to her. She cupped his face tenderly as he kissed her, grateful that she would experience this at least once, and with someone who had somehow carved a place within her heart.

No matter who won the contest she would still lose. The hopeless feeling grew worse with each passing day, and she wondered how she would bear it.

Wanting to forget the misery that awaited her, she focused on the feel of his tunic beneath her fingers. Thin summer wool, over a linen undertunic, and beneath that the hard plates of his muscular chest. Tracing the lines of his body with her hands, she sighed with pleasure.

In turn, his hands roamed her body, learning the shape of her. It was a leisurely exploration, and her curiosity was making her impatient. She pushed him back a little, until he lay on his back, and she leaned over him, her hand stealing underneath both tunics to the hot skin beneath.

She pressed hard, urgent kisses against his supple mouth, bending him to her will. In response he surged up to press her back down against the bed, his hands stroking her with a light and gentle touch. She moaned, half with pleasure and half with frustration.

Reaching up to grip his hair, she tugged him close, deepening the kiss and pressing her aching breasts against his body, desperate for release. His fingers plucked at the ties of her shift…the slippery cloth fell loosely around her collarbone, and he was able to pull it down enough to kiss the curve of her shoulder.

Dark hair brushed against her cheek and she shivered as he licked at her skin, soothing the scorching fire within. His mouth moved lower, and his fist tugged down the fabric to reveal one breast.

Cupping her flesh in his palm, he wrapped his lips around her nipple and sucked gently until her back arched like a bow. Raising one leg, she slid it over his thigh, encouraging him to do more, although she wasn't sure what. All that she knew was that she longed for more.

'Take these off,' she said, tugging at the hem of his tunics to grab his attention. Ulrik obligingly helped her by quickly peeling them off. The firelight flickered over his skin. Dark hair was scattered across his chest, tapering down to his stomach, and she stroked her hands down him, satisfied by the slight hitch in his breath as she did so.

Settling himself between her legs, he smoothed his hand up her thigh, gathering the thin fabric of her shift in his palm as he did so, until it was scrunched into ribbons around her hips. Stroking softly across her bare skin, he touched her intimately between her damp thighs, and she moaned, wrapping her arms around his neck and pulling him close, a little embarrassed by her body's immediate and intense reaction to him.

He was playing her like a lyre—the press of his chest, the sweep of his tongue, not to mention the stroke of his fingers, were all building a carnal rhythm inside of her that made her gasp as if she were drowning.

Eager to feel everything, she rocked her hips against his fingers, until the tightness within her became so strong that all she could do was whimper his name and place her trust in his confident hands.

Then she shattered, like a wave across the rocks, her body arching and then sinking back with a sigh of pleasured relief. As she waited to catch her breath he brushed his lips against her face and neck before rising up onto his elbows to look down at her with tender affection.

'We do not need to go any further,' he said kindly, and she stared up at him, still feeling shaken to her core.

Reaching up, she gripped his biceps, tugging him urgently down towards her as she arched to meet him. 'I want to experience all of it…with you.' He hesitated, and she knew he feared the repercussions she might face, so she added, 'Just once…'

It was enough to convince him, and he sank down into her embrace in a willing surrender.

Grabbing the hem of her shift, which was already bunched around her hips, she swept it off over her head, and then reached for the ties at his waist.

He turned away from her to pull off his trousers—

he must have kicked his boots off earlier because he was not wearing any now. As he undressed she noticed the gruesome scar across his thigh and winced.

'It is an ugly sight,' he said, and she shook her head.

'It is not the look of it that bothers me, but the pain… It must hurt terribly…even now…'

He rubbed at the knot of scar tissue. 'Sometimes.'

She took his hand in hers and tugged it. 'Come back to me,' she said, and it was a plea for him to leave the pain of his past behind, even if it was only for one night.

Lying down beside her, he gathered her into his embrace. This time his desire was more passionate, and she welcomed it gladly. Their kisses burned through them, building heat with every moment they spent in each other's arms.

The knowledge that this would be their one and only time together urged them forward with a wildness that consumed them. Astrid had seen naked men before—anyone that bathed in the fjord was used to seeing all manner of bodies, young and old. But she had not seen a man filled with lust before, and it excited her to see the power she held over him.

Reaching for him, she stroked his cock lightly, unsure of what to do, but so fascinated by the silky touch of him that she couldn't resist. He groaned, his voice husky and thick with desire, as he pushed against her and sought out her neck to bathe it with his tongue.

Shivering, she tugged on the back of his head to pull him up towards her mouth, wanting to breathe him in. His fingers slipped between her legs, and instinctively she curved her body to meet him. He let out a low and approving growl of pleasure when he felt her wetness, and then he was shifting his body to lie between her thighs.

Broad shoulders eclipsed the light from the fire as he raised himself up and over her. He braced his big arms either side of her head, and she knew it was to take his weight and ease the burden on his thighs. Running her hands over his muscles, she smiled in appreciation of his strength.

He pushed his hips forward slowly, and she reached down to guide him into her entrance. She gasped a little at the strange sensation of his filling her, and he pressed kisses against her face and neck as if to comfort her.

But she didn't need comfort. 'More!' she gasped, reaching for his hips and tugging him close.

He cursed against her neck, and she giggled. But the laughter turned into a cry of delight when he thrust his hips forward, and filled her completely.

His kisses became more urgent as he moved inside her, setting a steady rhythm that made her blood sing.

She clawed at his back, arching her hips and spine in a desperate attempt to increase the now familiar spiralling pleasure within.

'Astrid!' he begged, his voice hoarse. '*Princess…* You will break me too soon if you keep moving like that!'

On the brink of her own climax, she hissed in frustration, 'Don't call me Princess!'

Wrapping her legs around his hips, she pulled him close, burying him deep within her, as wave after wave of pleasure washed through her. Ulrik cursed as his body ignored the will of his mind, and his own release swept through him.

They lay entwined together for a long time, gently stroking one another in a bittersweet goodbye. When they heard a cart roll past signalling the start of a new day, Ulrik silently untangled himself from her bed, dressed and walked to the door.

'I wish you luck,' he said before he left, and she smiled, knowing that he meant every word.

There was nothing left to say—their fates would be determined at the autumn blot, and they both had plenty of work still to do.

Even so, Astrid pulled her blankets around her, as if she were protecting herself from a chill.

How could she go back to pretending there was nothing between them?

Except it was hopeless to expect anything more. When the contest was over, one of them would leave, and even though she cared for him she knew it could not be her.

How could she accept another man?

It would destroy her, especially now that she understood the marriage bed. She doubted any of the jarls her father wanted for her could compare to Ulrik. Even the idea of anyone else made her feel sick. A man like Bjarni? Never.

No, she had to win.

Chapter Seventeen

The twelve days of the midsummer festival passed quietly in the shipyard. Astrid and Ulrik worked on their figureheads in the empty camp during the long, peaceful days, quietly talking and laughing as they worked side by side. Before *nattmal* Bo would wander over to collect Astrid for the evening meal. It was part of her agreement with her parents that she would always be present.

Ulrik had taken to joining her. He said it was to prove he wasn't taking advantage of the extra carving time, but the truth was he wanted to reassure himself of her safety. So they would set down their tools and meet Bo halfway. During the meal, she would sit at the high table with her family, and scowl at every jarl who tried to speak with her, while Ulrik sat with the boat-builders and Frida, trying his best not to stare.

Afterwards he would walk her home, listening as she ranted about how awful or dull each of her suitors were. Slowly he began to realise what she had meant before.

'I am sorry,' he said after a particularly callous jarl had spent the entire night boasting to her about how strictly he punished his thralls.

'He will be the sorry one when his thralls eventually turn on him,' laughed Astrid.

'No, for when I scolded you for wishing you had been born poor.'

She blushed. 'That was stupid of me. I would rather be born as a worm than as one of Jarl Horik's thralls! You were right to remind me of my privileged position.'

'But I forgot about my own advantages.'

She smiled, reaching across and patting his cheek lightly. 'I will miss you, Ulrik. Maybe in another life we can both be worms.'

He laughed, and she stared at his face with a pained expression. 'I think I will miss these the most.' She prodded at the dips in his cheeks, and his smile dropped. 'Will you join me tonight?'

After that first night together, Ulrik had reinforced her door with bolts and made sure she was settled behind it each night before he went to his own bed. Of course, that did not stop Astrid from inviting him in, but each time he refused.

As always, she teased him when he shook his head.

'Ah, yes, *only once...such a pity.* Goodnight,' she said, before stepping into her longhouse and bolting the door.

They had not made love again. Ulrik knew it was for the best. It was what they had both agreed, but he worried over her. Astrid behaved as if she had already accepted her fate—whatever it may be. She carved her figurehead with diligent care, but there was a calm, sad resignation in her expression which had not been there before. As if she knew she would lose, regardless of who won the contest, and he was beginning to realise how wise she was.

They would both lose.

As they carved, Ulrik cherished their easy conversations. It was a time he would always remember as golden, pure happiness trapped in amber. They discussed methods, advised each other on designs and techniques, and debated the benefits of the Borre tradition against the Jelling style. They spoke of everything, except the future.

There had been a few times when he thought she wanted to talk about it, when she might have asked him for more without hiding behind her playful teasing. When her hands would linger on his while passing him a tool, and she would look at him with longing in her eyes. But then a grim determination would settle on her features, and he realised she was deliberately choosing to ignore her desires.

So he did the same, pushing his emotions down deep within, and quickly diverting her attention onto a less rocky path...like their work.

Astrid no longer viewed him as the enemy, and he was grateful for that, but there could be nothing more between them. One passionate night of madness could not change that, and he was miserably counting down the days until they would part for good.

Still, his eyes betrayed him, and whenever she was fixed on her own work, he found himself studying her face. The carving of Hel's beautiful side resembled Astrid more each day, and he had not even realised he was copying her until it was too late.

Astrid's serpent also began to take shape, a vicious, open-jawed beast with horns and a gruesome forked tongue. It was amusing to see such fine hands create such a terrible monster, and he wondered if she had been inspired by all the jarls she'd been forced to speak with. It was almost comforting to see her skill, because then she would not have to marry another. The idea of someone else spending their days and nights with Astrid filled him with bitter resentment.

He hoped she won for her own sake, so that she would know her worth and be proud. He no longer cared about winning—except for how it would benefit

Frida. If he were the victor… Could he really stand by as she was forced into a marriage she did not want? He was not a king, or even a jarl, so what could he do? And what if he put Frida's safety at risk?

Astrid glanced up at the hall, and then turned to him. 'We should probably go. Tonight is the last feast, and my mother will want me early for the wheel-burning.'

'Fine, let us go, then. I will be glad to have Frida home.'

'Have you missed her?' Astrid asked as she oiled and put away her tools.

'It has been strange without her. It has been the two of us for so long that the longhouse feels empty without her.'

Astrid gave him one of her dangerously teasing looks—how she loved to play with him even now. 'You did not need to spend every night alone…we could have made an exception…if you were lonely.'

He busied himself with putting away his own implements. 'No, and I think you agree with me, although you like to suggest otherwise.'

Astrid chuckled, and waited patiently for him to join her. As they began walking towards the hall he wondered if he should say more, warn her not to make such jests when the teams returned. But that might offend her. He had taken so much from her already, and he refused to take her pride as well.

It was clear when they arrived at the hall that the feasts had taken a heavy toll on the people—they did not retire as early as he and Astrid. Everyone looked exhausted, with dark smudges beneath their eyes and sallow skin. Many slept on benches, or were slumped against barrels. In comparison Astrid and Ulrik looked as fresh as spring water, but then they had not danced, wrestled, eaten and drunk themselves into the mud like the rest of the settlement.

As they entered the hall Frida came running up to her father. Ulrik swept her up into a tight embrace and hugged her fiercely. 'Have you grown in just one day?' he asked.

'No!' she laughed.

'You look as if you have grown a foot at least! Do you not think so, Astrid?'

Astrid's eyes widened for a moment before she examined Frida carefully, and then with a nod she said, 'I would say two feet, at least.'

It had taken him a moment to realise why she had been so surprised, and then it had hit him like a hammer: he had called her by her name.

'Our two masters grace us with their presence!' crowed Liv loudly. Astrid's sisters were sitting either side of the Queen, who appeared to be asleep in her throne, her head tilted to the side, her crown slightly askew on her head.

'I wonder, are you not sad to miss the fun we have been having? You always leave so early...' asked Bodil, and Liv cackled with a wicked look in her eye.

'Perhaps they were making their own fun? Tell me, *Astrid*, what have you been up to?'

Frida became tense in his arms, and instinctively he gathered her close. But there was nothing he could do to protect his daughter from their cruel words, especially ones he had invited with his own recklessness. The wall he had so carefully built between him and Astrid had crumbled, and cold dread washed through him as he realised how defenceless they all now were.

He had gone too far and put his child at risk.

'My figurehead is going well, thank you, Liv,' Astrid replied smoothly, before asking, 'Where is Father?'

Ulrik breathed a sigh of relief when he realised Astrid had spoken true—the King and most of the jarls were not present.

'They are at the bathhouse,' Bodil answered. 'We ladies are to use it after. Then the wheel ceremony will begin. Ahh, look—here they come!'

The King and the jarls entered, looking far more rejuvenated than those who had remained. Their skin glowed pink from the steam, they were laughing good-naturedly amongst themselves, and were dressed in elaborate, freshly laundered tunics.

'Oh, sorry you missed your turn to bathe, Ulrik!' cried Astrid, slapping her head with her palm. 'I should have remembered to tell you. It is a tradition on the last day of the feasting, and I completely forgot!'

'There was no need to tell me,' he replied, and he took Frida's elbow firmly. Ushering her towards one of the benches at the back of the hall, he told his daughter quietly, 'We must remember our place here, Frida. We are not one of them.'

Frida looked up at him and nodded. 'I know, Father.'

Of course she knew. He was the one who had forgotten.

Astrid may see him as an equal, but her family clearly did not. If the true intimacy of their relationship was ever discovered, Viggo could have him and Frida killed, and no one would stop him. Power was not a beast he should be toying with in his position, and Liv's words had reminded him of that. The knowledge grounded him, and set his thoughts in stone.

No more frivolity, no more pleasant conversations, and *definitely* no more teasing.

Astrid welcomed her father, but was quickly swept up with the other women as they prepared to go to the bathhouse. Not wanting to forget Ulrik and his daughter for the second time, she sought him out, and found him with Frida at the back of the hall.

'Frida, you will come with us to bathe, will you not?'

'It is probably best I stay here,' she answered.

'Nonsense!' laughed Astrid, grabbing her hand. But before she could pull her up, Ulrik's steely grip snapped around her wrist and stopped her firmly.

'No, she will stay here.'

Astrid's heart jolted with surprise at the unfamiliar tone. Never had he spoken to her with such indifference—anger, yes, but never this coldness. It scared her more than she liked to admit, and she released Frida with a hollow chuckle.

'But surely you will want to look your best for the wheel-burning?'

Frida smiled politely. 'I bathed this morning in the fjord with the others.'

'Oh, but that is not as nice at the bathhouse! We have oils and soaps from the east. Afterwards you will smell delicious, like a spiced cake!'

Frida hesitated, looking towards her father, who was already rising from his seat. 'No, *Princess*. She will stay with me from now on. Once the closing ceremony is complete, all will return to how it should be.'

Astrid felt as if he had ripped out her heart with that

one word, *Princess*. Had the last days meant nothing? She realised he could not risk sleeping with her again, but had grown to consider him as a friend. Obviously he was not, for why would he speak to her so coldly? Were they back to being enemies and rivals? She realised Liv's comments must have rattled him, but to dismiss her so quickly after all that they had shared…?

It felt…heartless.

Yes, she knew there could be nothing between them. That she had to focus on winning the contest, if she was at least going to keep her freedom. But did she have to go back to hating him? She didn't think she could, and it made her feel weak and pathetic to acknowledge it.

Straightening her spine, she glared up into his eyes. 'Fine. Do as you please,' she said, and walked away with as much pride as she could muster.

The hot bathhouse was not as enjoyable as it normally was. The chatter and laughter swamped her with an oppressive heat. Neither did she care for the fine silk-embellished gown she was dressed in.

The procession up to the ashes of the bonfire felt as if she were walking to her funeral, and she barely heard the long speech her father gave about the changing of the season. She helped collect some of the ashes with her sisters, pouring fistfuls of the dark powder into a large clay pot she had balanced on her hip. The ashes would be used again at the autumn blot to anoint the sacrificial offerings, and she played the part of princess dutifully.

She could not see Ulrik or any of her friends—they must be towards the back—and she scratched at her collar absently as she returned to her mother's side.

'Oh! You have marked your dress!' sighed her mother, brushing at the cloth with her elegant hand.

There was a natural lull in the ceremony, while the men rolled the giant wheel into position at the cliff's edge. Tar had been thrown over the wilting flowers, and it no longer looked quite so magnificent. However, it no longer needed to look pretty, it needed to burn, signalling the fall of the summer sun into the darkness of winter.

'Sorry,' Astrid mumbled, staring at the ground.

'Where's Frida?' asked her mother as she adjusted the silver crown upon her head. 'I have not seen her since the procession began.'

'With her father.'

'Ah, good, I expect she will return to the beach tonight.' When Astrid said nothing, she continued, 'I have grown fond of her. She is so…sensible.' Her mother played with Astrid's hair, artfully arranging the loose locks around her shoulders.

Astrid nodded, wondering if this was a subtle reprimand. 'She is.'

'Her father...is he the same?'

'I think he wishes he were.'

'But he is not?'

'Not at heart. I think he believes he must be...cautious. He is a parent after all.'

'Yes, that does change things.' Her mother nodded thoughtfully. 'Come, let us lead the procession, and say goodbye to the sun.'

Astrid swallowed down the unexpected tears that pricked at her eyes, and nodded. Each of her family took a torch from a warrior and lit the giant wheel. The tar lapped up the flames greedily and soon the whole wheel burned brightly.

Warriors moved forward with poles, and they began to push the wheel towards the cliff's edge. The voices of the crowd filling the air with chanting, as the wheel slowly creaked into place.

It teetered on the precipice, as if it were fighting not to fall, and then with a fiery hiss it rolled out of sight. Thuds and cracks flowed up as it bounced down the cliff, but all anyone could see was the scatter of sparks and smoke left in its absence, followed by a distant splash as it hit the water far below.

The crowd rushed forward, cheering, eager to

watch the burning sun extinguished by the waves beneath.

Astrid's feet refused to move. She didn't want to watch it die.

Chapter Eighteen

Ulrik sighed heavily at the two ships in the yard. It had been several weeks since the midsummer festival, and there was nothing more they could do to improve the structure of their boats. His was wide and low, like a fat-bellied whale, while Astrid's was smaller, with the sleek lines of a serpent.

He imagined Astrid would win the race, whilst his would take the load contest. But nothing was certain, and the days were getting shorter. The trees that would be bare in winter were beginning to yellow as cooler winds kissed them.

The autumn blot was fast approaching, but he was confident they would be ready in time. The masts were firmly set in the keelsons, and the steering oars were attached. Both ships were in the final stages. The teams worked on planking the deck and oar benches, while he and Astrid concentrated on their figureheads and decorations.

He should be grateful that the trickiest parts of the build were over, but if anything, he felt more restless. Sleep evaded him most nights, and when he did sleep he struggled to rise in the morning, despite there now being a clear distinction between night and day.

It was clear who was to blame, although he tried his best not to acknowledge it, even to himself.

For weeks he had tried to ignore her. Which later he realised was foolish—it had not worked previously, and only made her behaviour worse. Except this time her goal was not to make him angry, but instead to incite his lust. He would have rather been angry. Astrid seemed to delight in torturing him in all manner of increasingly imaginative ways.

It had all started when the team had returned from their midsummer celebrations. She had complained of the stifling heat, and had stripped down to only her undertunic and trousers as she worked. The sight of her lithe body so scantily clad was enough to send him into the forest to look for a suitable mast. Except she had insisted on joining him, claiming some nonsense about ensuring a fair choice.

The trip had been unbearable even though they were surrounded by the team. She had taken every opportunity to stretch or bend her body whenever she was near him in the most provocative of ways. Several times he had to walk away mid-conversation just to get his breathing under control, and when they returned to camp, he had taken his fishing boat out in the fjord until *nattmal* just to avoid the sight of her.

Unfortunately, that had only been the beginning. For weeks she had plagued him. Staring openly at him regularly, her eyes eating him up and spitting him out with knowing looks that fired his lust and embarrassment in equal measure.

The following week he had dropped his hammer on his foot simply from watching her drink from a flagon. She had laughed merrily at him, and he deliberately avoided working anywhere near her after that.

Of course, that did not satisfy her, and in the evenings she celebrated their achievements with ale and dancing, her body twirling in the fading light as she laughed and made jests with her friends.

He tried to ignore her, but it was almost impossible, and as the days dragged, his temper shortened. He became irritable and surly. Frida and his team stepped carefully around him, and blamed his bad humour on the upcoming competition.

Ulrik rolled his shoulders until his neck cracked, and wondered what new mischief Astrid would spin today.

Whatever she might have had planned was thrown aside when the King decided to check on their progress. Arriving with several warriors, Viggo took his time in examining each ship with a critical eye. The sculptures were placed in front of each ship ready to be raised and mounted. Astrid and Ulrik waited in silence by their figureheads for him to speak with them, and eventually he did.

When he came over, he wasted no time in explaining why he was there. 'They look almost complete.'

'They are,' replied Astrid.

'Good. King Olaf will be sailing here by the end of the week. So we will need to start the trials soon. Your mother has begun preparations for the autumn blot today. Will these be ready to sail in five days? I want the first two trials complete before he arrives.'

Astrid and Ulrik had glanced at each other—King Olaf was the man who would judge their figureheads in the upcoming trials. A silent nod passed between them, and Ulrik spoke to the King, 'We are ready.'

Viggo frowned. 'You two seem relaxed, considering the challenges ahead.'

Astrid shrugged. 'We have already done everything we can to build fine ships. A few more planks, some painting, and then we will both be complete.'

The King's eyes flowed over the two figureheads for a moment. 'Your serpent is impressive, Astrid.'

Astrid's eyes widened. 'Thank you, Father,' she said, and then laughed nervously. 'Are you well? It is not like you to pay me compliments.'

Viggo's gaze snapped to his daughter with clear disapproval. 'You have skill. I have never said you did not.' He frowned at Ulrik's figurehead. 'An unusual choice. Not what I would have picked, and quite… realistic in style… Perhaps King Olaf will like it.'

Astrid stepped forward and smiled at his sculpture. 'I rather like her. Does she not remind you of some-one, Father?'

Viggo tilted his head thoughtfully, and Ulrik's throat tightened painfully.

'It is Hel, is it not?' the King asked, and Ulrik gave a quick nod.

'Oh, but she is so lovingly carved…' Astrid leaned down, placing her face next to the figurehead, block-ing out the corrupt side of Hel, and showing the simi-larity of her own face to that of the goddess's beautiful side. Waves of fear washed through him as he won-dered what the King might think of such a daring similarity. Flattery or insult, either could lead to ruin, and, though he did not fear for himself, he worried for Frida.

The King's eyes narrowed, and he glanced at Ulrik before answering, 'Beautiful women are dangerous, Ulrik. Hopefully, Hel will guard you from them.'

Ulrik's shoulders slumped and he nodded with re-lief. If the King did see a similarity, he had chosen to ignore it.

Viggo left shortly after, looking in a sourer mood than when he had first arrived. Anger burned through him, and with his fists clenched he began to walk away. But Astrid's hand stopped him. 'I was only teasing,' she chuckled, her hold lingering long enough to squeeze his arm before releasing it.

If this had been the only time, he might have ignored her. But it was one of many, and even though each attack was small, this time it had been in front of her father, and it had cut deep into his jugular.

Wrapping his hand around her wrist, he tugged her between the two ships and pushed her against one of the frames so they were out of sight. *'Ormstunga!'* he snarled. He had never cursed at a woman before, but he had had enough of her serpent tongue. 'Enough of these petty, childish games!'

She gasped as her back thudded softly against the wood, and then a slow, sensual smile dawned across her face. 'There he is…' She reached up with her free hand and tenderly brushed a loose lock of hair from his eyes. 'There is the man I spent a passionate night with. I wondered where he had gone, or if I had imagined him. You have been so cold since…'

He grabbed the hand and forced it up against the hull of the ship. 'You are maddening!' he snapped, unsure of whether he wanted to shake or kiss her, and hating himself for both desires.

She let out a sigh of pleasure, her body going limp in his grip. 'I was afraid you no longer cared, or worse…that you never did.'

She sounded so sad, as if she really had missed him. It cooled some of his rage, and he released her. 'Is that why you tease and humiliate me in front of your father? I would rather go to him now and confess all, than live waiting for the death blow to fall.'

'Death blow?' she laughed. 'Do not exaggerate! I doubt my father would mind, unless it was made common knowledge…which it will not be.' The last part was said in a reprimanding tone, and he scrubbed a hand down his face in frustration.

'Then why imply it? Why flirt and tease me so openly? Have you no thought to how this may affect Frida? Do you hate me that much?'

'Hate?' For the first time she looked genuinely stunned. 'I did hate you for a time, but…' She dropped her head against the hull with a sigh. 'Now… I *want* you…to acknowledge that I exist, that we have feelings for one another, even if we can do nothing about them. I know it is madness, but I cannot stand to be ignored like this, as if nothing happened between us.'

The breath was knocked from his body and he took a step back. 'You are spoilt. You cannot have everything you want,' he grumbled.

She shook her head miserably. 'I know, but it still

hurts. We agreed it was only going to be the once…
But can we not at least be friends? You seem to have
spurned even that between us. I am sorry I teased
you. I only wanted you to see me again.'

Ulrik winced as if she had punched him in the gut.
'I am sorry. It was all such a terrible mistake. I never
meant to hurt you. I should never have—'

She interrupted him by raising her hand and pushing herself away from the hull to stand straight and
proud. 'No need to say anything more. Just know that
I do not hate you. The truth is, I never should have.'

'You had every right to hate me. I came to take
your position.'

'But that was not your choice, that was my father's.
Maybe that's why I was so focused on hating you
from the very start…because then I would blame him
less.'

Ulrik sighed.

What could he say, to make her feel better?

Her relationship with her father was strained at
best, and he could not understand Viggo's behaviour. If Frida wanted to work as a shipbuilder and
never marry, he would welcome her, grateful that they
would never be forced to part. But then, he was not
a king, and Frida regularly talked about wanting her
own children, so he doubted he would face such a
challenge.

Struggling to think of anything comforting to offer, he decided to rebuild their friendship instead. 'I think you will win the figurehead contest.'

Crossing her arms, Astrid stared at him with the same critical eye her father had used to examine their work. 'Not necessarily. Your depiction of Hel is stunning and unique. I particularly like her beautiful side.'

Ulrik glanced back at his figurehead with a smile. 'She is my best work…but a crude sketch in comparison to yours. The detail of your serpent is astounding—I swear you have magic running through your veins.'

'Thank you.' A rosy blush swept up Astrid's cheeks and he was mesmerised by it. Never had she looked so stunning, and it was all because he had complimented her. It made him feel like an ungrateful wretch for not doing so before.

She moved forward leisurely, and he fell into step beside her. 'I will no longer tease you, as long as you no longer ignore me.'

Ulrik gave a grim nod of thanks, but he could not speak. The truth was stuck in his throat like a chicken bone, because he also wanted her. Tormented by her very presence, he was already lost. She didn't need to flirt with him to consume him body and soul. If Frida would accept it, and if there was any chance her father would allow someone as low-born as himself as a suitor, he would have asked her to marry him after their night together.

But that was an impossible dream. She was as rare and special as a gem, and he didn't even have a silver coin to offer her.

'I suppose we should tar and paint the ships, ready for the challenges ahead,' said Astrid thoughtfully, and he was grateful for the turn in conversation.

'Let us split the paints—it will be easier to make only one batch of each colour.'

'That sounds like a good plan. I have a few more carvings to finish, especially at the back of my ship.' She pointed to the intricately forked tail at the back of her ship. 'But I should finish that by tomorrow. So, any colours you do not mix, I will make them.'

'You had time to decorate that as well?' Ulrik looked up at her stern and saw the intricate panels of engraved runes. He gave a low whistle of appreciation and shook his head. 'Why do I even bother?'

A river of scorching heat race down Astrid's neck. *Why did his words so affect her?*

But she had her answer when she saw the distant figures of her father and his men returning to the hall. Viggo's compliments were always begrudging at best, and sheathed in disapproval. 'Thank you,' she said quietly.

Ulrik frowned. 'I mean it.'

'I know, but thank you for saying it. Besides you will most likely win the cargo hold. Your ship is twice the size of mine.'

Ulrik tilted his head towards his boat. 'I will.'

Astrid laughed, his honesty a tonic to her soul. 'So it might all depend on the race.' She tapped the sleek belly of her hull. 'I wish you luck—you will need it!'

Ulrik chuckled. 'Your serpent is fast, but my lady is powerful. No one knows how well a ship will sail until she tastes the salt of the sea. No matter the design, a ship is like a lyre—it needs to be played before it can be truly called seaworthy.'

They said a good-natured farewell, and Astrid was sure the whole camp sagged with relief when they emerged from between the ships without bloody scratches.

It felt good to crack the ice that had formed between them. It was what she had longed for; his indifference had been unbearable, even though confessing it to him had been humiliating. A terrible weight had now been lifted from her shoulders, because now she knew why he had acted the way he had.

He was afraid for Frida, and she could understand that, although his reasoning was flawed.

Ulrik and Frida would face no consequences from that night, Astrid was certain of it. The only person who would be blamed was herself. It would prove to her mother and father how reckless and peculiar she truly was. She had denied men for years, only to fall into bed with her professed rival—even she had to admit it was ridiculous.

Virginity was highly valued in young brides, but she was certain her father would not care about the loss of hers. She had always been rebellious, and a princess was allowed certain indiscretions. Besides, her future husband could be easily compensated for it.

Viggo might even be glad of it. It would be the perfect excuse to rush her into a marriage with another jarl. Whilst her mother would argue it had ruined her for all marriage—not that she believed it—but she would say anything to oppose her husband. Astrid could imagine the raging battle of wills that would begin if she confessed what had happened, and it made her want to crawl under a rock and never come out.

Yes, she had teased Ulrik in front of her father, but she knew Viggo would only suspect him of admiring her. It would displease him, but only because it might affect Ulrik's desire to win the competition. Once he was reassured of their continued rivalry, he would not care.

She looked out at the horizon thoughtfully. The blanket of green forest was beginning to burn with patches of gold and red. The blot was coming, and Astrid welcomed it. Soon the uncertainty would end, and at least she had tasted true pleasure first.

No matter what happened, she would never regret her time with Ulrik. She had made her choices and would stand by them.

Let the will of the gods decide her fate, and she would try her best to bear the misery that followed.

Chapter Nineteen

The following days were filled with activity, the kingdom busy with the reaping of the final harvests, and storing food for winter. The warriors were out every day, hunting in the forests for boar. It was Frey's animal, and, as the god was associated with prosperity, the Queen wanted as many as possible for the upcoming feasts, whilst Astrid and Ulrik worked long days with their teams, finalising every detail on their ships.

To the Queen's delight the forest provided plenty of boar, as well as a few stags. The blood from them would be blessed at Frey's altar and mixed with the midsummer ashes. Then they would be used by the Queen to anoint the fallow fields, hopefully securing the god's favour for the upcoming winter and spring.

The autumn blot was normally less grand as a celebration, a nod of acknowledgment to the gods for the changing of the seasons. Winter could be a time of starvation and loss, so it was best to prepare well, spending their time and stores wisely. Normally the feasts were short, and held for the royal family only. But the shipbuilding challenge had put more weight and importance behind it this year, especially with the upcoming arrival of another king.

The first two tests would begin before King Olaf arrived. There was no need for him to judge those, as the winner of each would be clear for all to see. When the King did arrive, on the final day of feasting, the figureheads would be taken down and placed before him for judgement.

Astrid would have preferred it to be judged in situ on her ship, but her father had thought that unfair... probably because she had decorated so many other parts of her own ship, unlike Ulrik.

She brushed aside that disappointment, as her figurehead was still her greatest achievement so far. She smiled up at the two complete ships before her, the paint shining in the sunlight. Bright red, greens and golds adorned them, and Astrid was proud of the craftmanship and hard work that had gone into making both vessels.

The rare oaks had not gone to waste.

Today, both ships would be blessed and anointed by her mother, and it felt as though the whole settlement had gathered to watch the spectacle of the figureheads being mounted to each ship. Astrid and Ulrik both believed it would bring them bad luck to not sail with a figurehead, and so they had agreed to raise them.

Ulrik passed by her, a wide grin on his face. 'Ready?'

She nodded, her heart fluttering and not just because of the excitement of setting the figureheads into position.

Both teams used a pulley to lift the carvings into position. Each one weighed as much as a warrior, and they did not want to risk knocking or damaging them in the process.

There was no need to worry, however, as they slid onto the stern posts smoothly. A few nails were hammered in to keep them stable, but otherwise they could be removed without trouble.

Some kings and jarls insisted on removing them when entering the waters of their home, as they did not wish to startle the good spirits of their land. But those who did that tended to use much smaller figureheads. Viggo had never cared for such precautions, as he believed the spirits in the north were strong and brave, not easily daunted by the sight of a monster.

Astrid believed it was because her father found it a needless and annoying chore.

Her mother also came to stand beside her, a warm smile on her face. 'I am proud of you, daughter. It is a fine ship.' The praise made Astrid's heart swell with pride, at least until her mother whispered, 'We may beat your father, after all!'

She gave a weak smile in response, and tried to push down the rotten feeling her mother's words had provoked...

Was the idea of her winning truly so hopeless?

The Queen was no longer looking at her, she was smiling triumphantly at Viggo, who was busy congratulating Ulrik.

Oblivious to her daughter's soured mood, she stepped forward to where the gothi had set up an altar for the ritual. After much chanting, a bunch of hazel was dipped into the dark mixture set out in a flat soapstone dish. The Queen took the hazel and anointed each ship, while the crowd cheered.

With the ceremony complete, the only task left now was to launch the ships and sail them to the fishermens' jetty further down the beach.

She walked over to Ulrik, who thankfully had moved away from her father to shout orders to his men.

'Are you going to be on it when it hits the water?' she asked.

'Are you?'

She nodded with a teasing grin. 'Of course! Where else would I be?'

'The first challenge will be tomorrow. I hope you

have prepared yourself for the defeat.' Ulrik's eyes shone with glee and she could not help but smile.

'I have been thinking of the cargo-hold challenge, and I think my keel is so evenly balanced that she may take more weight than you think!'

'Hmm,' he said thoughtfully. 'I doubt it. But then, there is always a chance, I suppose. Just as I may have a chance in beating you in the race.'

'What? Are you mad? I grant you—I *may* struggle with the hold challenge. But not the race. My ship will be as quick as lightning, compared to your old nag.'

'Old nag?' Ulrik spluttered with indignation, although she could see the smile teasing at the corner of his lips. 'You may have made a pretty ship, but I have spent years sailing. We shall see how well your serpent rides the waves.'

Astrid was about to argue, but then she caught her father's gaze and decided against playing with that particular flame. 'We shall see…' she said, and then left to climb the rope ladder to her ship's deck.

The two teams were not enough to crew and launch each ship. So the crowd had to help, and logs were placed along the beach, and the frames that supported each ship were dismantled with axes, whilst the crowd supported the hull and began to push forward.

There was a satisfying rumble of wood as the ships

began to roll towards the beach. The crash as they hit the water was so satisfying that Astrid gave a loud whistle, and laughed when Ulrik returned it with his own. Soon they were pushed out into the shallows, and the water carried the weight of the hull.

Astrid strode around her deck, checking for any leaks or weaknesses, but found none. Soon the rest of the crew had joined her onboard, and as she had no experience *actually* running a ship, she waited for Revna to show her how it was done.

The older woman was thorough in her explanation. After sailing for some time and taking a few turns around the fjord, they settled across from Ulrik's ship at the fishermens' jetty. It was strange to think that she had spent most of her life building ships, never to have had much experience in sailing them.

It made her wonder what else she might be missing out on in life, and…more worryingly, if Ulrik might be able to win the race—after all, he certainly knew far more about sailing than she did.

'Actually, don't drop the anchor yet,' Astrid said, calling out to her crew. 'Let us do another loop first.' Dutifully they all returned to their positions, and the oars beat into the water once more. They would join the feast late tonight, but it would give her some peace to know that she would have no regrets, and that she had tried her best.

* * *

'She is still sailing,' said Frida quietly as she leaned towards her father to refill his horn of ale.

'What?' Ulrik asked, unsure if he had heard her correctly. How did she know what he had been thinking?

'You keep looking towards the hall doors. Astrid and her crew are the only ones not here. Although I think her father will insist they return soon.'

Ulrik looked towards the King, who was frowning at the doors with growing irritation.

'She is not experienced in running a ship, and it is beginning to get dark.'

'I do not think the King is worried about that,' Frida replied with a sigh, and he had to agree with her, although he said nothing.

A movement to the side of him caught his attention, and he stifled a groan as Brenna placed a basket of bread, and another jug of ale down beside him.

'Greetings, Ulrik and Frida,' she said, nodding with a polite smile towards his daughter. To his surprise Frida didn't return the gesture, which was odd, considering he had always taught her to treat everyone kindly. 'Your ship is most impressive, Ulrik. I am sure you will win the contest.'

'Thank you, Brenna, but we will have to wait and see who the gods favour.'

'The gods favour you, and I certainly hope you stay,' she replied, her eyes trailing over his face and body suggestively.

Ulrik took a sip of ale to hide his grimace, and afterwards he said, 'For the sake of my daughter, I hope you are right.'

'Did you think about what I asked of you?' Brenna asked softly, and for a moment he saw the fear beneath her bold words, and his pity for her returned.

'I did, but I am afraid I will have to disappoint you.'

Brenna gave a quick nod, a flush spreading high on her cheekbones. 'I understand. Thank you for your honesty.' She leaned forward, her voice low. 'Do not worry for your daughter. I doubt the King will allow Astrid to win... I hear he has King Olaf in mind for her—he would not let her go for anyone less... But you did not hear that from me.'

Brenna walked away, and he felt as if a rusty blade had been plunged beneath his ribs.

'You cannot trust her,' Frida whispered urgently, and he wondered how much she had overheard.

'Why not?'

Frida shook her head. 'I... I cannot say... It is just a feeling. And the Queen has said many times that King Olaf will be an honourable and fair judge. She has high hopes that Astrid will win the sculpting challenge. Brenna is lying because she is jealous of Astrid.'

'Why would she be jealous of Astrid?'

Did Frida know about himself and Astrid?

His stomach twisted into a clump of knots. What would his daughter think about such an odd match?

Frida looked away with a shrug. 'Because she is a thrall and Astrid is a princess.'

Ulrik frowned at the weak answer, but did not argue with her about it.

Frida was right. There was no way Viggo could ensure Astrid's defeat.

The winner of each challenge would be obvious, and he had also heard good things about King Olaf, that he was a ruler praised for his honesty and fairness…although would such a man remain impartial if a marriage alliance was offered as a bribe?

Still, Viggo might go against his word regardless of who won the contests.

Ulrik wondered, not for the first time, if the price of Frida's home was worth the same as Astrid's happiness. He was beginning to think it wasn't, and he felt wretched for even contemplating such a thing. It was his duty to provide for his daughter.

But that wasn't all—Brenna's words had troubled him in more ways than one.

He would not let her go for anything less.

It was a harsh reminder that even if Ulrik asked Astrid to marry him, her father would never accept anyone as low-born as himself.

They could never be together, but at least if Astrid won, she had a chance of being happy.

Chapter Twenty

It was the day of the first trial, and Ulrik ate porridge and cloudberries with Frida outside their home. A blanket of mist covered the water, and Frida looked at it thoughtfully.

'Is there bad weather coming?' she asked 'Do you think it will cause problems for the trials?'

'No, it will burn away. The days have been clear, and there is nothing to suggest that will change.'

Frida stirred her porridge. 'I see.'

Ulrik put down his bowl. 'Are you worried about the challenges? If the weather turns, it will be a good thing. Astrid is not experienced in running a ship in all weathers, I am, so it may give me the advantage.' For some reason, his words didn't seem to comfort either of them.

Did he no longer care about winning?

'I know,' she said with a light shrug.

'Are you worried? I will ensure you are safe and provided for, no matter what.'

Frida looked up at him, and he realised there were dark smudges beneath her eyes. He'd thought she'd seemed a little restless recently. But he'd been too exhausted himself to notice. The last push to complete the ships had meant his sleeping deeply each night, thanks also to the truce between him and Astrid.

Frida sighed, shifting forward on the bench, as if she wanted to say something but could not find the words.

'You doubt me?' he teased.

'No!' she cried, and then after a pause she said, 'Only…it has been nice. Living and working here with Astrid and the crews. It is a shame it will end soon, and it will, won't it? When the winner is declared. Either we will be forced to leave…or Astrid will be sent away.'

He nodded, and the porridge tasted like ash in his mouth. 'Yes.'

Frida sighed. 'I worry about what will become of her.'

That surprised him. 'You worry about Astrid? Are you not worried about what will become of us?'

Frida shook her head. 'I like it here, and I want to stay. But I am not scared if we have to leave. We can go back to Aalborg, or find a new place.' She leaned forward. 'I have been storing away some of our supplies, and if we must go we will not leave here empty-handed. We will be fine, whatever happens. We are resilient.'

Pride and love surged through his chest. 'You are the very best of your mother.'

Frida's eyes snapped to his, and her face lit up with pleasure. 'I am?'

He nodded, and for once there was no stabbing pain when he thought of her, only a bittersweet ache that was strangely comforting. 'She could make the best of any situation. She refused to accept defeat, and never let a mishap deter her.'

'I wish you talked about her more. Sometimes I worry you hate her—for what she did.'

He sucked in a sharp breath. 'For what she did?'

'You told her not to fix the roof, but she did it anyway, and then she fell. I worry that you hated her for it, for defying you.'

Was that why Frida always obeyed him so diligently?

It broke his heart.

'No,' he shook his head firmly, 'I blamed myself for not being well enough to help her.' He rubbed at his old wound absently, and Frida took his hand in hers.

'Mother prayed every night for you to get well. We were so grateful when you began to recover, but

you were still so weak, and we were so scared—'
Her words were choked by a sob and he pulled her
into his arms, as if she were a babe again, perched
on his knee.

'No need for that. I am here, and always will be.'

Frida hugged him back, and then brushed away her
tears with a lop-sided smile. 'I know. But please do
not blame yourself—Mother would have hated that.'

He fought the tears that threatened to spill from
his own eyes, and dragged her close, breathing in
the smell of her soft hair, and then with a shudder-
ing inhale he gave up the fight, and let the tears fall.

'She wouldn't want you to live alone,' Frida said a
moment later, her voice firm.

'I have you.'

Frida untangled herself, and began to gather up
their bowls. 'You know what I mean.'

'You do not stop loving someone just because they
have died,' he grumbled.

'The desire to love and be happy does not die either,' she replied, and sauntered back into their home
with a smug expression. 'You cannot use her loss as
an excuse, Father.'

'Where did you hear such nonsense?' he called
after her.

'Revna,' came her reply, and he cursed under his

breath, wondering when those two had become friends, and if, perhaps, they were right.

Of course, if he did take another wife, there was only one woman he wanted and he could never have her. But could he stand to watch her marry another? *Should he forfeit the contest? Deliberately lose?*

But he knew Astrid would hate him if he did that—she wanted to win fairly, and he would not diminish her triumph, or give Viggo the chance to claim it was an unworthy victory. Ulrik suspected the loading challenge would be his only easy win. He had no hope of winning the carving contest, but he might win the race. It would test his sailing skills, as Astrid had the faster ship, but she also lacked experience, and that could make all the difference.

So he would try his best, and give her the victory she deserved. If King Viggo went back on his word, Ulrik would not stand for it; he would rather forfeit and leave than steal her rightful place from her.

Frida's words had reassured him about their future. They *were* resilient, and together they would always survive and prosper. He had been wrong to doubt it, and at least now he could savour the challenges ahead, and be glad of Astrid's triumph when it came.

There was a strange peace in knowing that even though they could not be together, she would at least be free to live the life she had always wanted.

* * *

'The cargo load will be the first challenge,' announced King Viggo in a booming voice that carried down the fishermens' jetty to everyone gathered. Most of the settlement were present, as this would be an entertaining respite from the labour of the harvest.

Ulrik had heard that the challenges would be spaced out over the coming week to ensure there were no unnecessary interruptions in the gathering and storing of supplies. It was an unwelcome reminder to him that if he failed in this, he and Frida could very well be trying to find a new home during winter, which was less than ideal—even with her little hoard of supplies. Still, they would survive, he was sure of it.

Along the jetty were the many barrels of water, mead and ale all gathered from the stores, as well as the ale brought in from Astrid's sister. The Queen stepped forward, a piece of chalk in one hand, and an ornate staff in the other. He would guess she used it for religious ceremonies normally, but would use it to measure an equal load today.

Her voice was clear and carried far when she spoke 'I will mark the same length on each ship. When the boat sinks below the line, the load is complete.' The Queen marked each ship under the careful watch of the builders and the King, then stepped aside as the first crew began to load.

Ulrik had won the draw, and so he made quick work of organising his men. Each barrel was counted on a tally as it was loaded, and he was careful to ensure the distribution of weight was evenly loaded, otherwise there was a danger of the ship's capsizing.

Then as they approached the line of chalk, he ordered every man off and began to load them himself from the jetty, pushing them on one at a time, and being careful not to add his own weight in the process.

As each barrel rolled on there were collective gasps and hoots from the crowd. To his surprise he found himself thoroughly enjoying the spectacle, and he could tell by the grin on Astrid's face that she was doing the same.

Eventually his ship dipped below the chalk line, washing it away, and the barrels were checked and counted once more as they were removed.

Now it was Astrid's turn, and she had paid attention to his methods, because she did the same. She packed the ship so tightly he swore he could hear the timber groaning with dismay. Eventually, however, her ship also slipped beneath the line, and her tally was counted.

To her credit, he had only been able to fit five more barrels than her. It was not an unexpected victory, but Ulrik breathed a sigh of relief that he had managed to win one challenge at least. He could leave with his pride intact.

Viggo declared him the winner of the cargo contest with a joyous shout, and there was much back-slapping and cheers from him and his men. The Queen's praise was cold and stiff, but to his surprise Astrid appeared the most genuine in her congratulations.

She slapped his bicep, and said loudly, 'A well-deserved victory!'

'There are only five barrels between us.'

Astrid laughed, pointing towards her ship. 'But how will I go anywhere? There is no room to row!'

He chuckled with a nod of acknowledgement; he had at least left room for the rowers. 'There is that.'

Although disappointed, Astrid had been unsurprised to lose the loading part of the contest. She eased back against the wall of the hall and sipped her mead thoughtfully. Her father had begun the celebrations early, but she was too distracted to take the insult to heart. Besides, it was not solely due to Ulrik's victory.

Bodil was pregnant again, and thankfully the news had diverted her parents' attention for the moment. Her sisters and their families had arrived yesterday, with news that King Olaf was preparing to join them for the final feasting day.

In two days, the race would take place, and she knew that would be the true challenge. She had worked hard on creating an intricate sculpture that would impress the King, and she was pleased with how well it had turned out. Focusing her design on speed had given her an advantage for the race, but it had cost her the load challenge. However, she was not an experienced helmsman, and she hoped that would not lead to her downfall.

'Will you practise sailing your ship in the next two days?' asked her mother as she came to stand beside her, silver goblet in hand.

'I will,' she replied, straightening up from the wall, and feeling as if she had been caught sleeping when there were still chores to be done.

'Good, I shall ask Gorm to give you some advice, as he has been a helmsman for many years.'

Astrid nodded obediently. 'Thank you.'

'You would think he had already won, the way he keeps gloating!' snapped her mother waspishly.

'Ulrik? I think he has been quite humble about his success,' Astrid defended him quickly, a little surprised by the accusation. Her eyes were already seeking him out, and found him on a bench with Frida, laughing at the drunken axe-juggling of one of the warriors.

'No, I meant your father! He has been unbearable

all evening, and I do not think I can stomach any more of it!' She pinched her elbow, drawing Astrid's startled gaze back to her mother's narrowed eyes. 'You seem to admire your rival quite a lot. I hope there is no truth to those rumours your sister spoke of in the summer?'

'No!' Astrid gave a loud shriek of laughter that caused several people to glance their way, and she wondered if she had reacted a little *too* forcefully with her denial. Her heart was hammering in her chest like a wild horse, and she covered her blush by sipping deeply from her horn. Unfortunately, when she lowered it, her mother was still waiting for more. 'He deserved to win today. He will not win the sculpture contest, and I built my ship purposefully to be swift in the water… He has no chance.'

Her mother seemed appeased by her answer. 'That is good to hear. I always thought you had more sense than to be distracted by a pretty face.'

Astrid snorted, and was about to argue further when her mother raised her hand, silencing her.

'I have seen the way you look at him, and I am aware you have spent the night together.'

Astrid choked on her mead, and after struggling to catch her breath she whispered, 'How did you know?'

Her mother looked at her with bored disdain. 'You took preventative herbs from my stores.'

Astrid swallowed nervously. 'Does Father—?'

'Of course not! Although I would advise against letting it be known to him. He would only use it against you.' Her mother's gaze settled on Viggo across the room from them. He was banging his fist on the table, creating a beat, then his voice thundered out in a rich and deep song that tempted those around him to join in; they did so, and soon the whole room was filled with melody. A ghost of affection crossed her mother's face. 'Do not let your heart ruin your future.'

Astrid's head felt as heavy as her heart, but she nodded. 'It was only once... I wanted to know what it would be like, before I settled into my life as a boat-builder.'

Inga gave her cheek a light kiss. 'That is understandable, and he at least would have no cause to brag about it to your father. He would not dare.'

'Father would not punish him or Frida for it, would he? Or force me to marry him?'

'Sometimes you are so naive it hurts!' Inga gave a merry laugh. 'You think because he favours him today that he would forgive him such an insult? He would have him flogged and banished. The man is not your equal and could never hope to be...even if he was to become a master, your father would still not consider him. Instead, you will be sold off to some jarl's son for half your worth.' Her mother gave her a sharp look, and then tilted her head subtly in Ulrik and Frida's direction. 'So never speak of it again, for both their sakes.'

The Queen returned to sit at her husband's side, her face a mask of benevolent patience.

Astrid had had enough of company, and she was eager to leave the clamour and heat of the feast. Her mother's words descended over her like a storm cloud. Slipping from her position by the wall, she threaded through the crowd towards the entrance.

At least the jarls, like Bjarni, were no longer here— they had left after the midsummer feasts and not returned. There were still suitors of course, but Bjarni was not one of them, and she doubted her father had ever even considered him, had instead used him as a timely reminder. Telling her without words that he was King and the true power here.

She was surprised when Ulrik met her at the doors.

'Are you leaving? If you give me a moment, I can get Frida and join you.'

'No!' she cried, glancing behind her to check that they could not be seen through the crowd. 'I will be perfectly fine. Bjarni has gone back to his lands.'

'Still,' he smiled, and she realised his face was flushed and sleepy from drinking a little too much mead, and the effect was devastating to her already frayed nerves, 'it will be nice to walk back together—'

'No! There is no need!' She moved to the outside of the large open door, hoping to obscure herself from the people within.

'Is something wrong?' he asked, propping himself against the side of the door with his forearm. She could see a little carved hammer dangling from a piece of rope at his throat. When had he started wearing that?

Following her gaze, he reached for it, and fingered it lightly. 'It is for luck. I usually make one for Frida but she insisted I wear it instead.' He dug into his pocket, swaying a little, before pulling out a matching talisman. 'To make it fair, I made you one too. They are made from the wood of each of our keels—just a small fragment from the scrapped timber.'

A gift!

No man had ever given her a gift before. The jarls had talked endlessly about their wealth but had never offered something so simple and thoughtful as this.

It cracked something inside of her and she gasped. As if it weren't the sweetest present she had ever seen, it dangled limply from his clenched fist .

'The ribbon is silk,' then he added, 'A pri...a woman of your status cannot wear hemp against her skin.'

I should walk away, and not look back.

But the voice inside her head was not her heart. Her hand snatched the necklace greedily and then stuffed it into the purse on her belt. 'Thank you.'

His eyes widened at her sudden movement, but then he took a step back with a contented smile. 'Good, Frida said you would like it.'

The mention of Frida curdled the contents of her stomach, and she tried to sound brittle and cold when next she spoke. 'Good luck, Ulrik. I think you will need it!'

He smiled, and those dimples called to her. 'You are right, I am glad I have won one contest at least.' Then with a frown he warned. 'But do not be complacent.'

'I won't be,' she whispered, her chest tight, as he gave a brisk nod of approval.

'I will miss you…when I am gone.' His words were rough and deep, as if they had been pulled from his soul.

Tears filled her eyes, making it hard for her to see. 'As will I.'

Clearing her throat, she finally did as her good sense demanded, and strode home as fast as her feet could carry her. She didn't look back once, her hand resting gently over her purse, and the little hammer inside it.

Chapter Twenty-One

Astrid stood beside the steering oar of her ship with Revna, a drum and feathered baton in hand. They were waiting for both crews to take their positions so they could begin the race.

Revna licked her finger and held it up in the air. 'Are you going to row to the rock and then use the sail for the return?'

Astrid nodded absently, and watched as Ulrik's crew took their benches on the other side of the jetty. He had more men, because his ship was bigger and could cater for them. She had fewer, but the lighter weight of her ship would compensate for that.

Her eyes fell on Ulrik, who was watching her intently. Their eyes met for a moment and they both grinned at each other, their eyes bright with challenge and excitement.

He reached to his neck, pulled out his hammer and kissed it. Her heart melted like hot butter, and her hand instinctively touched the hammer lying against her breastbone. She had been careful to keep it concealed beneath the layers of her tunics, although she wasn't sure why, as no one would realise its significance but him. However, just like their one night together, she wanted to keep it safe and hidden.

To treasure it, as the gesture of love that it was, true and pure.

A pleased expression crossed his face, and then he turned away to order his men, ensuring as she had that his rowers were equally distributed for balance.

Her parents stood at the end of the jetty, the King with a signalling horn in his hand. When he blew it, the race would begin. Astrid focused on each step of preparation, trying not to allow her mind time to become too fogged up with fear. She had to concentrate on every moment. Gorm had been a good teacher, but he was old, and so he would not be joining her at the oars. Instead, she had Revna by her side, her second good-luck charm.

Viggo raised the horn to his lips, and the only sounds were the soft hiss of waves below, and the sigh of the wind above.

Then the wail of the horn sang out, and there was a collective guttural inhale as the rowers pulled on their oars. Revna began to beat her drum, and Astrid shouted encouragement.

The agreed route was to go out into the fjord, pass the central rock where it met the sea, and then return. The first figurehead to pass the end post of the jetty would be declared the winner.

The boat creaked and pulled away from the jetty with ease. She had practised the launch a hundred times in the last two days, hoping it would give them a substantial lead. Ulrik's boat was big and heavy, and it would take time to hit a steady rhythm.

Astrid's heart thundered in her chest as she glanced to the side of her. Ulrik's crew were pushing out into the water at an equal speed to her own. She glanced at Revna, who began to beat at a faster pace, and her crew strained to meet it.

Soon they were cutting through the waves cleanly, the prow bouncing as if it were a horse galloping and not a serpent. She chuckled with admiration when she saw Ulrik with Bo at the oars, shouting out a beat. It should not have surprised her really—Ulrik was a man of action, and she doubted anyone except him could match the blacksmith's strength. Frida sat at the steering oar, a steely determination in her eyes.

Ulrik had the advantage of strong men in his crew, and Astrid had always known he planned to use that against her, which was why she had worried less about the cargo hold, and more about the shape and light-ness of her vessel.

The distance between them began to stretch, but she cursed when she saw how well positioned Ulrik's ship was. She would either need to get closer, and risk hitting the rock, or go wide and allow Ulrik the advantage. She had not considered the position of her ship's approach in relation to another ship, and she would now pay for that oversight dearly.

No! I will fight and regret nothing.

She had learned many lessons from her time with Ulrik, but she remembered one in particular.

Work with your limitations and not only succeed, but also triumph.

'She can make it!' Astrid said beneath her breath, and then she pulled hard on the steering oar with all her might, carving a new path. The ship tilted dramatically to the side as it swept in a sharp arc between Ulrik's ship and the rock. Her ship was sleek and fast, and she trusted it to make the turn and not capsize.

'Oars in!' she yelled, and winced as she heard some of the oars clatter and scrape against the rock.

'Sail!' she screamed, and the crew in charge of the sail dragged in their oars, and rushed to the mast. The red and white sail unravelled with a snap, the rigging hissing and cracking like a whip.

The boat jerked as the wind hit the sail and propelled them forward, the serpent prow splitting the waves with a froth of sea foam. A cheer rang out from her crew as the ship righted itself, the hull dipping and soaring beneath her feet as if they were being pulled by a team of wild horses.

She allowed herself one last look at Ulrik's ship. He had moved to the steering oar, his sail unfurling and billowing as it caught the air.

This experience clarified what Ulrik had said, and she was glad she had taken the time to learn her ship.

'A ship is like a lyre—it needs to be played before it can be called seaworthy.'

Now she understood his words as she steered and shouted orders to her crew.

It was a living, breathing monster, and although she had always understood the reason to shape and curve certain pieces, the wind and sea gave them purpose and meaning. Now that she could see them in action, her mind was swamped with ideas for improvement, and refinement.

For the first time, she truly understood her ship—and herself.

What use were her skills if she did not use them? What was the use of her pride without independence? How could life have meaning without a heart?

The wood creaked and moaned, the hemp ropes rustling as they scratched through the rigging, and as they raced towards the shore she had never been prouder. Whether she lost or won, she would always be grateful for this moment, witnessing her beautiful monster come to life, and tasting true freedom.

Ulrik's team sailed a short distance behind, and it did not surprise her. It might have before, but now that she knew him better, she knew how close this contest would be. A skilled boat-builder and helmsman, Ulrik knew how to sail his ship to its best advantage.

Even now, it would still be a close call as to who would pass the final post first. Astrid called to her crew, her throat raw as she encouraged them to prepare to anchor, refusing to slow until they at least passed the end post. Then they threw out the anchor, and allowed the momentum of the ship to take them in while the anchor scraped the bottom of the sea, until they eventually ground to a halt with a vicious jerk.

Some of her crew fell to the deck, but no one was hurt. They rose to their feet with matching expressions of joy and triumph.

Astrid leapt from the boat and onto the jetty, stumbling forward as she ran to her father. Her heart hammered against her ribs like a frightened bird as she dropped to her knees before him and gasped, 'I did it! I won!'

Viggo said nothing, and instead looked over her

shoulder at Ulrik, who had only just anchored but was already making his way towards them, his limp barely visible.

Ulrik shook his head with a smile. 'It was close. But your ship is impossible to beat, Astrid. She is as swift as lightning.'

There was a moment of silence, and Astrid feared her father would think up some excuse to steal her victory from her. Her mother stood beside him, her knuckles white as she gripped her folded hands in front of her. A tight smile stretched across her face as she, too, waited for the King's judgement.

'Well done, Astrid.' The words were surprisingly tender, and when she looked up there was a soft smile on his face. Her stomach tightened, and she felt tears prick at the backs of her eyes.

Her father reached down and stroked the side of her cheek tenderly. 'You did it.' There was a strange sadness in his eyes for a moment, and then he pulled away, turning to the crowd, and slapping his meaty hands together in a loud clap.

'Come, let us all drink and feast together. Celebrate my daughter's first successful challenge!'

Her mother took her by the elbow, helping her to her feet. Cupping Astrid's face in both hands, she gave her a hard kiss on each side of her face. 'You were magnificent!'

The King and his warriors were already halfway down the jetty, and heading towards the hall. Ulrik came to her side, and gave her a congratulatory pat on the shoulder.

'Be proud,' was all he said.

'King Olaf will be here in the next day or so,' said Viggo. 'You will need to remove your figureheads tomorrow and place them outside of the hall. The ships should be moved back to the shipyard. So be merry, eat and drink your fill. Soon you will learn the name of my master shipbuilder!'

Astrid raised her horn to a resounding cheer. *'Skol!'* she shouted with the rest of the crowd.

'A dancing song!' cried her mother, and the musicians obeyed with a spirited melody.

Astrid gave a shocked yelp when her mother grabbed her hand and pulled her into the centre of the hall.

'Dance with me, daughter! Soon you will be too busy with your shipbuilding to feast with me!'

'Hush!' giggled Astrid. 'Nothing is certain!' She glanced towards her father, who was talking amongst his friends. Thankfully he had not heard, or was not willing to hear them. It still astonished Astrid that he had not seemed daunted by Ulrik's loss today.

'How can you lose? Your figurehead is the most

impressive beast I have ever seen!' Her mother was slurring her words, her crown a little lop-sided on her head as she twirled around the room, one hand gripping her skirts, while the other was looped around her daughter's elbow.

Astrid was still wearing her manly clothing from the race, and nobody—including her father—seemed to care.

Maybe he had finally accepted that he could no longer control her?

Mother and daughter twirled together, until her sisters joined them, and then Astrid gratefully slipped away. The strong ale had made her dizzy, and she was gasping for breath as she slumped against one of the pillars.

A dark shadow blocked the light from the mounted torch, and she looked up to see Ulrik beside her. 'I should probably say my farewells now,' he said, although he did not seem upset by such a prospect. She wished she could say the same about herself.

'What?' She stepped away from the pillar, cold dread washing through her followed by a choking pain. 'Why?'

'Do you honestly think I have any chance of winning now?' It sounded as if he was teasing her, and she frowned, staring at his mild-mannered expression, and wondering what secrets lay beneath.

'There is still the judgement of the figureheads—you have to wait for King Olaf to arrive!' Panic gripped her in its icy claws and she wanted to beg him never to leave, even though such a desire was impossible...or was it? She was beginning to wonder.

'As if that matters any more.' His eyes captured hers, and she saw flames dance within. 'None of it matters, not to me.'

Her throat tightened, and then she slapped him playfully on his arm, afraid that she had read more into his words than was there. 'Of course it matters! Both of our teams have put so much time and effort in, and...*we* have worked hard. I wish to know the winner!'

'Fine!' grumbled Ulrik with a begrudging smile, which, as always, made him look devastatingly handsome. 'But I wager you will be the winner!'

She leaned closer. 'And I wager it will be you!' She stabbed him in the middle of his chest with her finger. It took all her effort not to linger on the touch.

At his disbelieving look, she shook her head. 'I admit my carvings are elaborate and intricate in their beauty. But the idea behind yours is unique. There is no other like it. Maybe King Olaf would prefer that? I do. I would pick yours over mine. Some people value what is rare and different, rather than what is expected.'

His eyes seemed to devour her. 'True, but yours is still better,' and then he leaned forward and whispered, 'I need to tell you something.'

Chapter Twenty-Two

'What?' Astrid stared up at him wide-eyed, and he cursed his impatience—he should have told her when walking her home. The timing was not ideal, as they were surrounded by revellers, and only a short distance away from the King.

But neither could he let go of Brenna's words. He had deliberately sat close to Viggo's chief warriors, hoping he might learn of any plot to marry off Astrid by force or deceit. Unfortunately, he had heard nothing to suggest Brenna had spoken the truth, but he would never forgive himself if he did not at least warn her.

He spoke carefully, his eyes searching for anyone who might be listening, but found no one. 'There is a rumour that when King Olaf arrives your father means for you to marry him, whether you win or not.'

A pained expression crossed Astrid's face but it

was quickly smoothed away. He wished more than anything that Brenna was lying.

'It is only idle talk, and there may be nothing to it. But I thought you should know. He may use you as a bribe to encourage Olaf to cheat when judging the figureheads.'

Astrid sighed miserably. 'I will tell my mother, and she will insist he give a fair ruling. She might even insist he judge the figureheads as soon as he arrives…my father won't be able to tell him which one to choose then. But…honestly, I know King Olaf personally, and he is an honourable man, especially when it comes to oaths. If he swears to judge fairly, he will. I doubt even my father could bribe him out of keeping his word. So do not worry.'

Ulrik suddenly felt helpless. 'But…what if he does? What if he fails to choose your sculpture as the best?'

Astrid's head tilted, and she stared up at him in disbelief. 'Then you will win, and become the master boat-builder… You and Frida will be able to stay. You wanted to stay, did you not? To have a home here? If I am to be sold like a broodmare, then at least it will be for a good reason!'

'Not at the cost of your freedom. I would rather leave now than take that risk.'

Her eyes widened, and she took a step closer. The

smell of wood shavings and eastern hair oils filled his nose and intoxicated him. 'Most would disagree with you. Except possibly my mother…oh, and my sisters. They will be furious—a king! When they could only manage a jarl… They will be sick with jealousy, so that will be some comfort to me at least.' She chuckled as if it was a great jest, and his blood hummed in his ears. He grabbed her arm and tugged her into a darkened corner of the hall, as far away from prying eyes as he could manage.

'Be serious, Astrid!' he hissed.

She rested a hand against his chest, her eyes kind. 'Everything will be well. Maybe…it will be for the best. Frida deserves a home, and I know she will be happy here. And if I lose, I will lie and agree to choose a man. Not the King, but a jarl, ideally one who lives far away, and will take many weeks to arrive…although, of course, I won't be waiting. I will walk into the mountains, and most likely never return.'

'How can you say that?' he asked, horrified, and she waved it away as if it were nothing.

'Let us leave it in the hands of the gods, and…*my mother*,' she giggled, and he realised she was a little merry from the ale.

He leaned forward and examined her closely; her eyes were clear and bright, so she still had her wits.

Taking a deep breath, he for once dared to be careless. 'I only wish you could come with me.'

'You *wish* I could come with you?' she asked, her precious lips becoming a perfect circle.

He nodded, realising too late how close they were, how *temptingly* close. 'I know there is no future for us. But I want you to know, you have my heart all the same.'

'Your heart?'

'Damn it, Astrid! Must you make me repeat everything I say?'

'If you continue to make very little sense, then yes, *I must!*'

'I had thought that if you at least won—'

'Do not pretend you are going to *allow* it!' she snapped angrily.

'I did not mean it like that!' he retorted, and then hissed a foul curse and grabbed her hand. He tugged her through the crowd until they were outside in the cool night air.

It was still not far enough away for him. The voices from inside were still loud, and the flickering lights from within the hall seemed far too close. He swiftly moved to the side of the hall, and into the darkness, dragging her with him.

Breathless, he turned and stopped her before she ploughed into the back of him with the firm grip of his hands on her shoulders. He could barely see her, the moonlight his only guide, and he cupped her face in his hands and leaned forward.

'You deserve to win. It is the only certainty in all of this, and I will happily accept our parting if it means that you are free. Frida and I will be fine whatever happens—I realise that now. But if you are forced to marry someone you do not love…' He struggled to find the right words. 'I could not bear it.'

His whole body ached with longing, and he was unable to resist her. He pressed forward, crushing his lips against hers. She gasped, stumbling a couple of steps backwards, and he pressed his body forward, pushing her against the wall to steady them both.

Her mouth felt so right against his, and his tongue teased hers as he gasped for breath. 'Not only because it would pain me to know you are someone else's wife.' He pressed his lips against hers, tasting her with feverish longing. 'But also because I know such a marriage would kill a part of you. The bright, creative and joyful part of your spirit that I love so dearly!' he gasped against her hot mouth. His skin burned with desire as he said the words he had kept so tightly chained within. He barely recognised his own voice it was so husky. 'I am driven mad by you daily. You consume all my thoughts. You are both infuriating and impressive in equal measure. I love you, with all of my broken heart and soul.'

She melted against him, her arms winding around his neck, and he had never wanted to claim a woman so desperately in his life. But she remained silent and he feared she was already lost to him.

How could he ever hope to compete with a king, or be strong enough to defy another?

'I wish there was a chance for us,' he whispered. 'But I will accept defeat, as long as I know you are happy.'

There was a desperate look in her eyes as she cupped his face in her hands. 'How can I be happy without you? I love you too.'

A bittersweet joy filled his chest. 'Eventually, you will be… I promise. As long as you have your craft and your independence.' Unable to offer her any more words of comfort, he could do nothing more than kiss her, hard and thoroughly, and she matched him with her passion, a silent agreement passing between them to savour their last moments together.

Her hands fumbled beneath his tunics, exploring his skin, and trailing fire all over his chest. Eager to check that she was ready for him, he deepened the kiss and undid the ties of her belt. Pushing his hand down beneath the fabric, he groaned with delight when he found her wet beneath his fingertips.

She rocked her hips against him, moaning. 'I have longed for this…every day…since the first time.'

She pulled at his hair, tugging his mouth back to hers.

'As have I,' he murmured, and they each gasped for more air and more of each other.

She began to fumble at the ties of his own waist, and he glanced around at their surroundings to check their privacy. No one was nearby, and they were slightly obscured by the animal pens towards the front of the hall.

'Shall we go back to our camp?' he asked, even as his knees felt weak, and he wondered if his heart would ever beat at a normal speed again.

'No, best not. Father said he wanted everyone to stay until after the skald had recited the sagas.'

He broke away from her, already regretting it as her sly hand reached down beneath his clothing to grip his manhood. 'Should we…go back to the camp?' he panted, the air catching in his throat when she began to slide her hand up and down him.

'No… If we are missing for only a short time he will not notice,' she replied, and even in the moonlight he could see the seductive mischief in her eyes. 'We must be quick.'

The pumping of her wrist increased in speed until he had to push her against the wall with a guttural curse, pinning her hand above her head. 'It will be quicker than either of us want if you keep doing that!'

She giggled, and he dipped his head to press kisses against her neck, his hand trailing down her arm to her ribs as his other hand snaked up the inside of her tunic to cup her breast. Her giggles faded into soft moans as his touch became more intimate.

Wiggling her hips, she let her trousers fall to the ground and was able to step out of them. Standing on one foot, she wrapped one leg around his hip and tugged him close.

Holding her thigh with one hand, he held her firmly and rocked his hips into hers, but not quite enough to enter her. Her back arched like a bow, and he took her nipple into his mouth with a gentle kiss. Her answering moan was enough to make him thrust her against the wall, and it eased some of the ache between his thighs, but he was quickly losing control.

'Are you sure?' he asked once more, conscious that this would be their second time together, and already things were on the precipice of no return.

He had to shift his weight a little from his bad leg, but he managed to balance them both.

'Yes!' Astrid pulled his mouth to hers as she fumbled with his trousers to release him. 'One last time,' she sighed, and he gathered her close.

His length was in her hands, the fabric of his trousers bunching around the swell of his bottom. He pressed forward, sliding at first his tip, and then the full length of him into her body. She sighed as he entered her, as if his body gave her some kind of relief, and then she squirmed against him, and there was no peace for either of them.

Filling his palms with her hips and backside, he thrust forward. Another dance began in the hall, and they were free to pant and moan each other's names. The drums started to beat loudly from within the hall and the sound muffled their cries of pleasure.

Ulrik met their beat, and soon they were wrapped in each other's arms, rocking to the rhythm that flowed around them. Astrid gripped his rump and urged him on, until finally she splintered beneath him in a rush of hot wetness that shattered his own tightly wound composure.

Moaning, he collapsed against her, filling her with his seed, even as he clung to her tightly. The chaos of the last few moments had left him drained and weak. But Astrid did not seem to mind; she giggled beneath him, even as he waited for his breathing to return to normal.

Eventually he found the strength to peel himself away from her, and they began to return their clothing to some semblance of order.

A sudden shout pierced the night, causing them both to jump.

'Fire!'

Chapter Twenty-Three

Astrid and Ulrik stumbled out into the clearing in front of the hall. No one seemed to notice them coming from the side of it, as the crowd spilling out from the open doors was too focused on Revna's cries. Sweat was pouring from her brow, and her breathing was heavy as if she had run a great distance.

There were only two words that could clear a hall so swiftly. One was *attack*. The other *fire*. Both could devastate a community in a heartbeat.

'Fire!' Revna shouted again, as if she feared no one had understood her, which was unsurprising considering how hoarse her voice was. She pointed behind her to the shore.

Astrid followed her finger, but it was not pointing at the shipyard, where Revna must have run from, but at somewhere closer. At first Astrid almost dismissed it as one of her mother's autumn bonfires, as it was too contained to be a barn fire.

But then a terrible realisation hit her.

A ship was on fire!

Viggo strode through the crowd. 'Where?' he demanded.

'The jetty!' Revna's wild eyes found Astrid's and they were filled with pity. 'Your ship is burning!'

Shock crashed into horror, and with a thundering heart she began to run, knowing from the pain in her friend's eyes that it was already too late.

As she ran, she prayed for the gods to be merciful. If it was just a section, then maybe she could rebuild, or at least save part of it.

The figurehead... It is my best work!

Please! Please! Please...

Her feet seemed to beat to the rhythm of her begging, and she arrived well before the rest of the settlement.

Poor Bo and Skadi were trying their best to quench the flames. They stood in the shallows throwing pails of sea water up and onto the burning ship. It had come away from its anchor, and had grounded in the shallows. If it had floated out further into the fjord, they would have been helpless to do anything at all.

However, despite the constant stream of water being thrown, the entire deck was engulfed in flames. Numbly Astrid realised some of the water around the hull was burning. Such a thing would only happen if oil or tar had been used deliberately to start the fire in the first place.

Someone wanted it gone.

The once magnificent dragon ship looked as if it were screaming through the roar of smoke, the polished wood blackened with soot and tarnished by the heat, the perfect oak from the rare and beautiful glade disappearing before her eyes.

More people joined them, and although they tried to throw water on the flames, all could see that the damage was already done. The sail her sister had spent months making was gone, and only a few flaming rags remained clinging to the mast.

It was a funeral ship now, a wasteful sacrifice, and her rage burned with it.

'No!' Grabbing a nearby axe that had been left amongst a wood pile, determined to save one thing at least, Astrid strode out into the shallows. Her eyes were firmly fixed on the figurehead, not realising she was crying until her tears scalded her cheeks.

Someone shouted her name, and she thought it might have been Ulrik. But she ignored it, and kept moving. The water lapped at her waist, and she dipped under for a moment, hoping it might protect her from the worst of it. Then she began to climb, using the axe to help her gain a foothold higher up—there was no good in caring about the hull now.

The gods would not steal her greatest work from her. The figurehead could be removed, but it would be far too heavy and time-consuming for her to lift it. Instead, she would cut it down like a tree. Once it was in the water, she could drag it to shore.

The smoke was suffocating. As she leapt into the body of the ship, she immediately began to cough and choke, struggling to catch her breath in the acrid stench of the burning tar.

Keeping her body low, because the air seemed a little less murky there, she forged ahead. Determination gave her strength as she clambered up onto the stern, and ignored the flaming deck that cracked and crumbled under a river of flame only a few feet away.

She swung her axe, and the shock of the blow sent a tremor of pain up her hands and arms. Ignoring it, she swung again and again, bracing her leg high on the prow for balance as she slowly chipped through the bottom of the figurehead.

Unable to hear anything over the roar of the inferno, she did not realise that the rest of the settlement watched her from the beach. She did not hear her mother's screams begging for her to return.

The mast fell with a deafening crack, falling to the side and shattering the hull with a cloud of burning shards. Astrid flinched as the ship surged up and then down as if in a terrible storm. Luckily, she had connected her axe at that moment, and only had to cling on to its handle to stop herself from being thrown into the air.

However, when she tried to pull it free, it refused to move, and she began to tug on it with all her might. Either she was losing her strength, or the death rattle of the ship had sunk it deeper into the wood. Astrid suspected it was a little of both.

Out of the billowing smoke, callused hands joined hers on the handle of the axe.

Ulrik had come to her aid.

She suspected he would have been here sooner if it weren't for his leg.

Combining their power, they managed to pull out the axe swiftly.

With a grim expression, he took the axe from her and shouted, 'Get out, I will do it!'

Astrid moved aside, but remained aboard, and with a curse at her stubbornness he swung the axe with a mighty whack. The figurehead tilted, and Ulrik thrust both hands against it. The remaining timber cracked, and then the serpent was tumbling into the inky depths below.

'Jump!' he shouted at her, pushing her towards the edge.

'Together!' She grabbed his hand, pulling him close. Then they leapt out and into the water. A deafening crack filled the air as the strong keel split beneath them. It was the final blow and the hull began to sink to its watery grave. The black fog of smoke parted beneath their feet as their bodies fell, and then they were swallowed by the fjord.

Astrid fought to reach the surface, realising that the ship had drifted further out whilst she had been trying to save her figurehead. She and Ulrik would have some distance to swim before they reached the shore. Ulrik's head came spluttering up next to hers.

Worried that he might find it harder to swim with his wounded leg, she quickly grabbed the figurehead which was floating nearby and pushed it towards him. He grabbed it gratefully, and the two of them swam with it towards the shallows.

Once they could feel the bottom with their feet, they began to walk, pushing the large sculpture as far as they could, until with a curse Ulrik's leg gave way beneath him and he fell to one knee amongst the pebbles.

Astrid was exhausted, and dropped down beside him. Looping one arm protectively around Ulrik's shoulders, she rested her head on her sculpture, and sobbed.

When the pain in his leg subsided a little, Ulrik looked up to search the crowd for his daughter. She stood beside Revna and the Queen, amongst the crowd of people who were watching the spectacle from the beach.

Frida gave him a small wave to show that she had seen him, a sad but relieved smile upon her face, glad to have them both return safely, but full of sympathy for Astrid, and what she had lost. Frida had urged him to rescue her, and although he would have done so anyway, it was reassuring that Frida had also been worried for her.

Viggo and Bo waded out to them, and the King grabbed his daughter's elbow and dragged her to her feet. 'Odin's teeth, Astrid! What were you thinking? Not only endangering yourself, but Ulrik too! He has a child that depends on him! Are you so selfish that you cannot see the consequences of your actions?'

Astrid flinched at his words, and she glanced at Ulrik with a flash of regret.

Bo silently stepped forward, and began to drag the figurehead towards the beach, the wood scraping against the shingle beneath.

Viggo's foot slammed down on it with a heavy splash. 'Is this really worth more than a life to you?' the King shouted in disgust, jerking Astrid's shoulder with a rough shake.

She shook her head pitifully, her tears breaking into a gut-wrenching sob that had him rising to his feet.

The smoke had burned Ulrik's throat, but he ignored the pain and croaked, 'It was my decision to help her. I would have done the same if it were my ship burning.'

Viggo scowled at him, but removed his foot from the sculpture. Ulrik helped Bo and some other men carry it to shore. He glanced at Astrid as he passed, and gave her what he hoped was a reassuring smile—the flood of her tears had slowed to a trickle at least. It pained him that he could not offer any more comfort than that. But it was impossible in front of her father. The cruel truth was that Ulrik had *already* toyed with his life…by bedding her.

How could he pretend her actions were any less rash than his own?

After depositing the figurehead safely on dry land, he turned and watched as the last remnants of her boat disappeared beneath the waves.

How fragile and fleeting their lives were.

All Astrid's hopes and dreams had been lovingly carved into that ship, and now it was gone.

How could her father scold her for trying to save a small part of it?

Rather than criticise her impulsive spirit as he might have done in the past, Ulrik admired her for it. At least she lived with the full depth of her soul, and without regret.

An unsettling thought plagued him, and he prayed his suspicions were wrong.

The fact that his boat was still moored at the fishing jetty, and remained untouched, seemed almost obscene in comparison to what Astrid had suffered.

Why had his not been burned? Or the jetty even scorched a little?

Unless Astrid's had been cut from its anchor, and then deliberately set alight?

Surely Viggo would not deliberately hurt his daughter like this?

Ulrik could never imagine doing something so cruel to Frida.

The Queen stepped forward and hugged her daughter tightly. 'Oh, my darling, I am so sorry.'

Astrid pushed forward, almost fighting her mother's embrace, as she called out to her father, 'The final test is based on the figurehead. I can still show it to King Olaf... All is not lost... Not yet!'

Her mother shook her head, and Ulrik knew as well as her mother that the challenge was over. Astrid just hadn't accepted it yet...or the truth about who had burned it.

Viggo glared at his daughter, his voice clipped and full of authority. 'Enough of this madness! You have no ship. How can you be declared the winner of anything?'

'But we have tested the ships. Ulrik won the load and I won the race. It is just the figureheads now, and I still have it!'

Viggo's patience seemed to snap and he bellowed, 'Who cares whose lump of wood is the prettiest? The competition is *over!* You have forfeited the final challenge. You have *lost*, Astrid! Allow yourself some dignity, and accept the will of the gods!'

'The will of the *gods*?' hissed Queen Inga, stepping forward with her fists clenched, and Ulrik noticed how several warriors suddenly looked uneasy. 'You *dare* to call this the will of the gods?'

Chapter Twenty-Four

Dawn was beginning to peek over the horizon, and some of the crowd carried torches, but it was nothing compared to the blazing light of rage in her mother's eyes. Astrid wanted to run and never return. She knew who had set fire to her ship. But a part of her loved her father, and could not accept what he had done. Hearing it spoken aloud would only make it real, and the pain far greater.

Inga stepped forward and looked at her husband with pure disgust, as if he were a dog that had made a mess in her bed. '*Dignity?* You dare speak of dignity when you treat our youngest so cruelly? You know full well who torched her ship! *You did it!*'

Viggo glanced towards Astrid, but could not meet her eyes. 'Why would I? I have lost a beautiful ship worth a fortune. *And* I have been by your side all night, *wife,* so watch your tone… Besides, there were others who were absent during the feast… Ulrik for one, and we all know the rivalry between him and our daughter.'

A new welt bloomed across Astrid's heart at the final betrayal. She had wondered how her father's reputation could remain unsullied after such a crime. The contest was a lie—neither of them was meant to win—and she had been too blinded by her pride to realise it until it was too late. 'Of course,' she sighed, but no one was listening to her. The crowd had turned to stare at Ulrik with angry suspicion.

A warm blanket was draped around her shoulders. It was Revna, and she gave her shoulders a light squeeze, before whispering, 'It was not Ulrik.'

Astrid patted her hand with a grim nod. 'I know.'

Revna stepped back, her expression filled with so much love and kindness that Astrid feared she would start weeping again. But her father's proud voice drew her attention back to him.

'I can understand it to some extent. No one would wish to lose to a woman!' laughed Viggo, but only his warriors laughed with him.

Ulrik stepped forward, and Astrid shook her head subtly. She prayed he would not reveal they had been alone together, as it would only lead to his further punishment. Already she was terrified about what her father would demand from him.

'On my honour, I did not torch it,' said Ulrik

firmly. But already the crowd, as well as her mother, had decided he was the one to blame. It was probably easier for them to blame a stranger than their own king.

But Ulrik didn't seem to care about the false accusation. Instead, he watched her with raw pity in his eyes. Astrid's hurt had become his burden.

'Were you afraid I would win?' she asked, her voice hoarse, and although she had deliberately looked at her father when she spoke, Viggo pretended she was asking Ulrik that question.

'I am sure he was,' he sighed, quickly moving away from her dismissively. His voice carried across the fjord as he passed his judgement. 'Ulrik, as we have a blood bond, I will let you and your daughter leave freely. I will even pay you handsomely for the build of the ship, but only if you leave *immediately*...' He cut the purse from his belt and tossed it at Ulrik's feet. 'Here is enough silver to see you and your daughter through the winter. I wish you well, now *go*.'

Ulrik stared down at the purse, and the silver spilling from it. It was a fortune for a man of his status.

Frida was the first to move. 'I will gather our things...' she said quietly.

'No!' Astrid cried sharply, and Frida paused. Turning to the King, Astrid tried to speak calmly. 'It wasn't Ulrik...it was *you*. I was talking to you, Father. Were you afraid that I would win? Would that truly have been *so* terrible?'

Viggo's eyes turned to chips of ice, and the threat was clear in the rumble of his voice. '*Ulrik* burned your ship. Your ridiculous behaviour drove him to it. I heard of your tricks and games! You have been spoilt and selfish for long enough. You *will* marry and Ulrik *will* leave. *That* is my decision.'

Her mother tried to argue. 'Surely you cannot hold her to that bargain—'

But Viggo's voice interrupted her like a clap of thunder. '*Enough!* You are to blame for this, filling her head with nonsense! She will marry, for her own protection and to no longer be a burden on this family. *That* is my ruling as her father and as her King!'

Her mother looked as if she was about to scream; her face paled and then reddened. Soon they would fight like two dogs over scraps.

It was exhausting, unsurprising and hopeless.

Astrid wanted to run and hide. She felt like a little girl again, desperate to find a place, a home, where she could be herself. Carving had been that for her once, but now even that would be taken from her. She was a weapon that her parents would take turns wielding against one another.

Ulrik remained where he was, the coins untouched

at his feet, his gaze never leaving hers. It looked as if he was waiting for something. Numbly she realised he was waiting for her.

'I will name the man I marry!' she snapped. 'And then you will *never* again have a say in my life, or what I do with it.'

Her parents stared at her, shocked by her apparent change of heart. Even her father looked surprised, despite his ruling.

'Well, yes… King Olaf is the man I have in mind for you, but if there is another jarl, then tell me his name, and I will send for him immediately.'

As Viggo spoke she reached for her Thor's hammer, and pulled it out from beneath her tunic. Holding it tightly, she met Ulrik's eyes in silent question.

Did he remember what she had said?

That she would pretend to accept a man from her father's stable—a jarl who would need to travel far from his lands. But that she would not wait for his arrival, and instead, she would walk out into the woods, and never return.

Let the mountains take her. At least then she would be free, and Ulrik could leave safely with Frida. Winter was fast approaching, and they would need the silver to survive.

Silently she begged him to pick up the coins.

A heartbeat passed, and then another.

* * *

Ulrik understood what Astrid was asking of him—
to take the silver and leave. He also knew that she
would not accept any marriage not of her choosing.
Instead she would leave her fate in the hands of the
gods.

No one would go with her into the mountains. She
would be on her own, without family or friends. No
one to stand by her side, to protect or defend her when
the harsh winds blew.

He could not stand it.

'Forgive me, Frida' he whispered, but he did not see
his daughter's reaction to his words. He was staring at
Astrid, pleading with her to accept him. He stepped
forward, over the fallen coins, and reached up to hold
the matching pendant at his neck.

'She will have me, or no one else,' he declared, and
the royal family stared at him as if he was mad. Even
Astrid gasped in shock, but he knew he had made
the right decision, and there was no going back for
either of them.

'*Ulrik?*' Her father choked out his name as if it
were rotten meat.

Tears swam in Astrid's eyes, and then she nodded.
'Ulrik is the only one I will accept.'

'*He burned your ship!*' cried her mother in outrage.
'You cannot trust him. You may think you can—but

you can't! Believe me, no matter what he has told you—'

Her father seemed to slowly realise the significance of the Queen's words, and his face turned purple with fury. 'What is the meaning of this?'

Ulrik spoke loudly so that no one could doubt his words. 'I did not burn Astrid's ship. I could not, because we were alone together, and if she wants me for her husband... I will prove my honour.' He glanced at Frida, fearing what she would think of his next words, and was surprised by the smile of confidence she gave him. It gave him courage to plough onwards. 'I will fight any warrior or jarl of your choosing. First blood wins. Let the gods decide if I am a liar, or worthy of a princess's hand.'

The King strode forward, until only the weak light of dawn stood between them. 'With axe and shield?'

Ulrik nodded. First blood with axe and shield could only mean death or at the very least serious injury— like the one that had crippled his leg. 'Yes, but I would ask that the Queen be allowed to take charge of my daughter if I should fall.'

'Granted! I like the girl, and will not hold the stupidity of her father against her,' replied the Queen sharply, and then with a softer tone, she added, 'She may even keep the silver you so foolishly ignored.'

Ulrik breathed a sigh of relief; all he wanted was to ensure Frida would be safe.

Unfortunately, Viggo was not done. 'Then sharpen your axe. For you will be fighting me, *old friend*.'

'Father, no!' shouted Astrid, and his heart broke. How could he even contemplate killing her father? Yes, the man had been cruel, but Astrid still loved him.

'You would ask me to kill the father of my future wife?'

'Why not? I will gladly kill my daughter's lover.' Viggo turned away from him. 'Bring me my axe and shield!'

Astrid ran to his side, and he felt as if they were still on her burning ship.

'I will not kill your father. I will disarm him, I swear it.'

Astrid shook her head miserably. 'You should have taken the silver and left!'

'Sometimes we must be brave and reckless to achieve our dreams—you taught me that. Let us trust in the will of the gods.'

'This is hopeless.'

'Life has been good to me; I met you, didn't I? I would not trade that for all the silver in the world.' For once, the unfairness of life did not bother him.

'I love you,' Astrid whispered, and she sank into

his embrace, not seeming to care about the people who watched them, including her parents.

Ulrik kissed the top of her head. 'I love you too, Princess.' He spoke quietly into her hair. 'If I fail, promise me you will not go into the mountains alone. Take my fishing boat and sail away with Frida. We are a resilient family, so you will be fine, even without me.'

'Am I part of your family?' Astrid asked, and she sounded so fragile. He wished that he could take every moment of pain that she'd suffered, and replace them with kisses.

'I have already lost one wife. I refuse to lose another. Do you promise to go with Frida?'

Her voice was rough with tears when she replied, 'I will, I swear it.' But then she looked up at him with that fiery determination he had come to love, and said firmly, 'But try your best *not* to die. My father is old, but he still raids regularly, and can fell even the strongest of warriors. Do not be stupid!'

Chapter Twenty-Five

The crowd gathered in a circle in front of the workshops. Viggo's axe and shield were quickly brought down from the hall. The shield was ornately carved with protective runes that Astrid had engraved herself, and was passed to the King with great ceremony.

Whilst Ulrik merely went into his longhouse, and brought out a simple, dusty shield, and his big battleaxe. It was the one Astrid had seen when he'd come to protect her from Bjarni.

She made her way to her father and begged, 'End this, please!'

'I will,' he raised his axe and thumped it against his shield, 'with his death!'

'But you wanted me to marry!'

Viggo's eyes narrowed, but he ignored her and stepped forward into the ring.

'Mother, I beg you!' Astrid entreated, but the Queen shook her head.

'I told you he would not accept it!'

'Make him! If anyone can make him see reason, it is you! You are his Queen!'

'Your father listens to no one but himself! Now, stay silent. We may be lucky and only lose your father this day.'

Astrid glared at her mother, not finding any amusement in her dark humour. 'Ulrik will not kill him; he knows it will only hurt me if he does.'

'Then let us hope he dies quickly. For you know your father will not be as thoughtful.'

Astrid prayed to Thor and Freya, clutching her carving tightly in her arms. Frida came to stand by her side and Astrid gathered her close, one arm around her trembling shoulders.

'I am so sorry, Frida!'

But Frida shook her head. 'It is my fault. I prayed to the gods that he would find love again.'

Tears rolled down Astrid's face as she kissed the top of hair. 'They heard both our prayers then, so let us hope they protect us now.'

The two men began to circle one another, shields pressed tightly to their chests, the axe handles supple in their hands. Viggo was the first to strike, and he lurched forward, hammering down on Ulrik's shield with a blow that would have floored a lesser man.

'I can't watch!' Frida gasped, leaning into Astrid's embrace.

'You should, child,' said Inga with a wry smile. 'Your father is doing surprisingly well.'

Astrid had to admit her mother was right. Despite Ulrik's injury, he matched Viggo's blows with equal force, often using his axe to hook them away. He could not move gracefully on his feet like other men, but he made up for it with his upper body strength and relentless power.

Unfortunately, Ulrik's shield was old and weak in comparison to the King's. Viggo took advantage, raining down blows repeatedly until the lesser shield splintered and crumbled.

Viggo stepped away, enjoying the spectacle of his approaching triumph. Ulrik threw the useless tatters of his shield away, and held his axe firmly with two hands.

Viggo moved forward once more, and with a mighty swing Ulrik swept down with his axe as if he were felling a tree. Thankfully, he had turned the blade of his axe, so that instead of cutting him down it merely swept the King off his feet, throwing him up and into the air. Viggo landed on his back with a heavy thud, his shield rolling helplessly away as he lost his grip on it.

It could so easily have been followed by a death

blow. But Ulrik stood firm, and watched as Astrid's winded father sucked in a dazed breath.

'I do not want to kill you!' Ulrik growled. 'You are my King!'

'You must, or I will keep going until you are dead!' Violent anger flushed her father's face until he was as red as the hair on his head. The grip on both their axes tightened, and Astrid swallowed her breath as she waited for the fight to begin again.

'Enough!' Inga shouted, sprinting forward. She grabbed the King's shield even as it was still rolling on the ground, and then dived between the two men.

'What are you doing? How dare you interfere? I can kill him myself!' Viggo yelled as he struggled to sit up. But Inga pressed him down firmly with her hand, even as she raised the shield high to protect him.

'First blood!' Inga yanked haphazardly at Viggo's trouser leg, having to lower her shield slightly to do so. When she raised it, she revealed a tiny cut, where the back of Ulrik's axe must have grazed him. 'Ulrik, you *are* innocent!'

Viggo cursed. 'That is—'

'First blood!' Inga thrust her palm down so hard on her husband's chest that he dropped once more into the mud. 'We may never know who really burned Astrid's ship,' she snarled, a dangerous look in her eye, 'but Ulrik has won. *That* is my ruling!'

Husband and wife glared at each other for a long moment, and then with gritted teeth Viggo nodded. Dropping his axe, Ulrik offered his hand to the Queen, who used it to stand. Her father was less gracious and stumbled to his feet with a scowl.

As her mother returned to her side, Astrid caught the glint of a needle being slipped back into the purse at her mother's belt. It seemed Astrid and her father weren't the only ones full of tricks.

'He is not worthy of her!' Viggo snapped angrily at his wife's back. 'How can you accept a man so far beneath her?'

'You do not have to accept it!' Astrid shouted, her hand firmly in Frida's as she went to stand by Ulrik's side.

'You will need my approval if you are to live here.'

'Then we will not live here,' Ulrik replied smoothly, and Astrid nodded, reaching with her free hand for his.

The warmth of his fingers gave her strength. 'You have no say in my life from now on, Father. I will gladly give up the life of a princess to be with the man I love.'

'Love?' Viggo gave a bitter laugh. 'And how long will that last during a harsh winter?'

Inga sighed, brushing the dirt from her skirts. 'If it is his status that bothers you, husband, then change it. Make him a jarl—you have the power to do so. Give him Bjarni's position…it would serve that wretch right!'

Viggo looked thoughtful for a moment. 'Perhaps.'

'No,' Ulrik said, and Astrid glanced up at him in surprise.

Would he really reject such an opportunity?

It appeared he would.

'We wish to become master boat-builders—the best ship makers in Viken and beyond! We will win fame and fortune for you in a way that no jarl ever could. You have seen our work. Imagine how impressive our ships will be once we have combined our talents. People will come from far and wide to commission a ship from our boat yard!'

'Impossible. No daughter of mine—' blustered Viggo, but Inga held up her hand to silence him.

'She is happy. Do not push her away from us any more than you already have!'

'Inga!' Viggo growled her name like a warning. 'You know all that I have ever wanted is to see Astrid's future settled, like those of our other daughters. She is too wild. She needs the protection of a rich husband, and the stability of a family of her own. That is what I have always wanted. *You,* of all people, know how vulnerable a lone woman is in this world.'

Inga's eyes flared with resentment at his words. 'Is that why you wished to force her into marriage? To tame her spirit, as you did mine?'

'I know you wanted her to love someone. But how has that helped us in our marriage? Your love for me grew cold as soon as you had to bend to my will. You resented the power I took from you...'

Inga stepped forward and poked her husband square in the chest. 'I have always loved you, and still do! It is true that I struggled at first. But you did not help, constantly leaving me to further your own ambitions! When you did return you expected me to immediately bow at your feet, as if I had not ruled in your absence for months on end. I needed time, but no sooner was I settled than you would leave me, *again!* Usually with a babe in my belly that you would not see until after it was born!'

Viggo stared in astonishment at his wife's words. 'Then... I am sorry for that. I thought you preferred it when I was away, and honestly, I feared losing you. I was a minor king before we married. I thought that if I built up enough wealth and power, you would see that I was worthy of you.'

Inga smiled, and cupped her husband's face lovingly. 'There is nothing to prove. I chose you for my husband, did I not? And I have never regretted it, even when you vex me with your arrogance and callousness!' She slapped at his face, but it was done lovingly with gentle pats.

With a sigh, Viggo turned to them and asked Astrid bad-temperedly, 'Do you *really* wish to marry a craftsman?'

'Why not? He is my husband in all other ways,' replied Astrid with a grin. Her parents' words of reconciliation had given her hope.

Even when the night seemed endless, there was always hope that the sun would return.

Ulrik inwardly groaned as Viggo's eyes settled on him with murderous intent. But to his relief, it seemed the King no longer wished to fight with him. He suspected the heartfelt conversation he had had with his wife was the reason for it.

The Queen shrugged. 'You wanted a match for her, and she has chosen.'

'Fine. I want you married before the end of the week,' the King ordered, and then he left with the Queen and his warriors as if nothing had happened.

The crowd began to disperse towards the hall, searching for food after such an eventful night and morning.

Ulrik's heart felt as if it would burst from his chest,

it was so overflowing with joy. Blue eyes that matched the sea turned towards him. 'Did he just give us permission to marry and live here as boat-builders?'

Ulrik laughed, and wondered if he would ever stop smiling. 'I think he did...'

With a shriek of excitement, Astrid and Frida both jumped up into his arms, and the three of them hugged each other fiercely.

Revna, Bo and Skadi joined them with warm smiles and words of congratulation.

'You must be hungry and exhausted after everything,' said Revna.

Frida practically bounced towards the campfire. 'I will make some porridge, and then you two should go and rest.'

Revna gestured to the hall with her chin, and chuckled to herself. 'The gods have been kind. I never expected your parents to reunite over you.'

Astrid shook her head with a disbelieving smile. 'I am as shocked as you are.'

'It is good—they are too old for such nonsense!'

'I am sorry,' said Bo, and Ulrik could see the guilt on his friend's face.

'Did Viggo order you to torch it?' Ulrik asked.

Bo shook his head. 'No, it was probably one of his warriors. But Astrid, you muist know...he did regret it. He ordered me to put out the flames. But it was already too late…'

'Bo tried…we both did. The King ordered us not to tell you… Can you ever forgive us?' added Skadi.

Astrid gathered her friends in a tight embrace. 'I am lucky to have you. There is nothing to forgive.'

When she eventually broke away from them, and Ulrik couldn't resist whispering in her ear, 'I did not think I could love you any more than I do…but it appears you keep proving me wrong, Princess.'

She smiled up at him. 'When I marry you, I will no longer be a princess.'

'To me, you always will be.'

Astrid hugged his waist tightly. 'I never thought I would like hearing that.'

Later, they gathered around the campfire and ate porridge together. Friends, family, and lovers. They laughed and talked about the future. Nobody noticed or cared about the burned remnants of the dragon ship that washed up onto the shore.

It did not matter because they had each other.

Perhaps they had unknowingly made a worthy sacrifice to the gods?

After all, the gods seemed to have favoured them since. Ulrik would be grateful to them forever, and consider himself lucky from this day forward.

Who could have imagined that Astrid—who had

hated him so fiercely at the start—would come to love him with equal passion?

Certainly not Ulrik.

Epilogue

Two years later

'They're growing well,' said Ulrik as he moved to Astrid's side and encircled her in his strong arms.

Astrid leaned back into her husband's warm embrace with a relaxed sigh. 'Our great-grandchildren will one day play in the shade of them.'

'Sooner than we expect, if Frida's army of suitors is anything to go by.'

Astrid chuckled at Ulrik's grumbling. 'She is a sensible young woman. She will wait until she is ready.'

Ulrik leaned down and kissed her cheek. She rather liked the idea of their family walking through this oak grove for generations to come.

The trees were tiny sprouts, barely out of the undergrowth of fallen leaves, and everyone had to be careful not to step on them, but enough of the saplings had established to replace the oaks that had been cut down. Sometimes Ulrik and Astrid would come here solely to cut down any encroaching pine or undergrowth that endangered the young trees.

'We should hurry, or we won't be back before nightfall,' said Frida, running past them and up the hillside, her basket filled with gifts from the Queen.

Astrid was glad they had decided to build their new boat yard further away from her parents' settlement. They were on the other side of the forest in a small inlet, not far from Revna and her family's farm. She loved her parents, but found she appreciated them more with some distance between them.

They were only half a day away on foot, but life was calmer outside the heart of the kingdom, and they could focus on their work in peace. Although they were never lonely, as many of the shipbuilders now lived at the boat yard with their families too. Farms and workshops sprang up around them, and each year it had grown a little larger. Soon it would be considered a settlement in its own right.

Astrid took Ulrik's hand as they climbed to the crest of the ridge.

'Do you remember falling down this hill with me?' she asked lightly, and he chuckled in response.

'I remember you falling, and taking me with you!'

'Come, there is something I want you to see,' she

said, hurrying forward excitedly. 'I think I have seen the right tree for jarl Sven's new ship.'

'I was hoping to rest before we started another!' Ulrik grumbled half-heartedly.

'Stop moaning—we should be grateful for the silver!'

Ulrik's lips twitched at her censure. 'We are already richer than we could have ever imagined!'

Astrid could not argue with that; they had not been without work since King Olaf had visited and seen Ulrik's ship and Astrid's figurehead. Viggo had had to gift Ulrik's ship to him, as compensation for the wasted journey—he had thought he was claiming a bride, and had not known of the contest at all. But in a strange way it had worked in their favour. King Viggo was now widely known as possessing the best shipbuilders to ever walk Midgard, and people came from far and wide to own a ship crafted by the undisputed masters.

Taking her husband's hand, Astrid tugged him forward. 'Down there!' she crowed. 'Isn't it perfect?' She pointed to a majestic pine on the hillside.

Ulrik only glanced at the tree for a moment. 'It is perfect,' he said, and then his eyes flowed over the view below them…

To their impressive boat yard with Astrid's figurehead mounted on the jetty, and then up to where Frida was clambering down the mountain path humming happily to herself.

Finally, his eyes rose to meet those of his wife. His mouth widened into a heart-stopping smile that showed off his dimples beautifully, and then he reached up and cupped her face, brushing a gentle kiss across her lips. 'Life is perfect.'

Astrid had to agree with him. Life *was* perfect.

* * * * *

COMING SOON!

We really hope you enjoyed reading this book. If you're looking for more romance be sure to head to the shops when new books are available on

Thursday 31st August

To see which titles are coming soon, please visit

millsandboon.co.uk/nextmonth

MILLS & BOON

MILLS & BOON ®

Coming next month

THE WARRIOR'S RELUCTANT WIFE
Lissa Morgan

'Peredur?'

He froze, turned, and caught his breath. One of the shapes had risen up in the bed and, despite the dimness of the room, he knew it wasn't the maid. Even if the tiring woman would never have addressed him by his name, he recognized Rhianon's voice, her slender form, the cascading fall of her hair.

'I was making sure the fire still burned,' he whispered, startled at the hoarseness of his voice. 'Go back to sleep.'

'What hour is it?'

'What hour?' Peredur shook his head at the strange question. 'I know not. Does it matter?'

There was a little silence. 'No, not really.' Another silence. 'It's just...there are no church bells here to mark the passing of the night.'

Through the dark, the flames picked out the curve of her cheek, the bridge of her nose, her wide brow. Her face seemed paler, her eyes bigger, her lips fuller.

'No, there are no bells,' he responded, his pulse beginning to beat a little faster as the firelight danced at the base of her throat. 'But it must be well past midnight.'

He'd studied her face keenly enough, as they'd sat before that other brazier, on that other midnight, their wedding night. But he hadn't seen her in a shift then, as he did now, nor beheld the smooth, bare skin of her arms. And now, his imagination proceeded to paint a vivid picture of the naked body *below* the shift.

Continue reading
THE WARRIOR'S RELUCTANT WIFE
Lissa Morgan

Available next month
www.millsandboon.co.uk

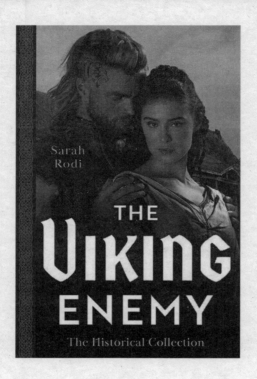